Hello &
for

LIKE
REAL

It's A FUN BOOK. If you agree, please
consider leaving a review somewhere —
or posting A pic on the socials

SHELLY LYONS

Shelly Lyons

Facebook/MIZLYONS   IG = mizlyonshere

TWIT =
dollterror13

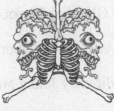

Thank
you!

Tiktok = ↑ same

Shelly Lyons
oops

Hope you Enjoy!

Ghoulish Books
an imprint of Perpetual Motion Machine Publishing
San Antonio, Texas

www.GhoulishBooks.com

Cover by Luke Spooner

Copy Edited by Jenna Malcolm

For Jordan Gallader, the dreamiest writer and danger girl I've ever accompanied on mad adventures or locked out of my house. You would have loved this story, darling.

LIKE REAL,
LIKE WOOOOO!!!

A Historical Introooo by John Skipp

YOU NEVER KNOW how you'll meet the friends who also wind up being artists you will champion for life.

For me—in the strange case of Shelly Lyons, who YOU are about to meet—it all started on Facebook.

On this particular day in early 2019, I was sitting on my smoking porch in this awesome hippie house overlooking downtown Los Angeles, rattlin' off one of a trillion "informative" posts about writing, creative philosophy, and such (as I was wont to do). And the subject this time was "How to Turn a Screenplay Into a Novel".

It was a step-by-step guide about how to take your screenplay, strip out all the fancy formatting, change present tense to past tense, put the dialogue in quotations, put the prose into paragraphs, and break the scenes into chapters.

As I said in the post, this should only take about four hours. And if you do it right, by the end, you'll be left with *a really short, shitty novel*.

But if the blueprint of your screenplay was sound—if the characters were vivid, the dialogue was good, the plot was entertaining and the story moved—then the architecture of the book should be solid, as well.

JOHN SKIPP

Then all you had to do is go in and fill ALL THE INNUMERABLE BLANKS that the movie's director, stars, stunt people, production designers, cinematographers, grips, gaffers, fx people, makeup people, wardrobe people, editors, sound designers, *ad infinitum* would ordinarily take care of, in the process of making the film.

Because that's the difference between writing a book and a movie. In the book, the writer has to do ALL of that shit, using nothing but words to put the moving pictures in your head. A screenplay is a set of instructions. A novel (at its best) is a fully-formed organism. All it needs is a reader, and it's ready to go.

Well, as fate would have it, my dear friend Sabrina Kaleta (the "diva of Pasadena", as she shall be forever known) was also good friends with this crazy Shelly person. And by some algorithmic alchemy, Sabrina's response brought the post to Shelly's attention.

Evidently, it rang a bell. Because the next thing I knew, I had a message from Shell in my PMs, saying, "You don't know me, but I want to learn how to do that. You should teach a class. You should do it RIGHT NOW."

And for the next eight months, that's exactly what I did, starting the very next week. Very quickly, we had a handful of smart, excellent students who wanted to tell stories. And as the weeks went by, it winnowed down to four. Then it winnowed down to three.

In the end, there was Brian Asman, in the very last stages before his career hit the indie stratosphere. He generated so much kickass material so quickly that we were pretty sure there were five of him. Brain-damaged superhero horror. Bizarro science fiction. You name it, he was writing it, and writing it well.

And then there was Shelly, who had all these great unproduced screenplays piling up on her shelves (as is so often the case with screenwriters). And she had this one crazy-ass story in particular that we all fell in love with. A script she'd never quite finished. Had never quite parsed the end.

INTRODUCTION

So we broke the story down beat-for-beat, on files cards strewn across my hippie living room floor. Worked through the issues. Detangled the end. And then she set about doing the hard part. Which was actually writing the book.

And so, every week, she would show up with new pages. And every week, Brian and I would be laughing our asses off, going, "This is fucking GREAT!" and thanking our lucky stars that we got to be there from the very beginning.

As such, I am beyond delighted to introduce you to this beyond-delightful book: a first-class cyber-blast of lunatic frenzy and laugh-out-loud bizarro thrills. I love these characters, their preposterous shenanigans, every crazy goddam thing that comes out of their mouths. I love how the plot twists like a rubber Moebius pretzel. I love how structurally sound the story is, because she was a fine screenwriter to begin with.

And I love my friend Shelly Lyons, who is a great fucking writer. One of the funniest I know, as you're about to find out.

Is she the female Jeff Strand? DON'T MAKE ME PICTURE FEMALE JEFF STRAND! But if I said it, it's not an inapt comparison. She's weird. She's a hoot. She's got a fierce will to entertain, and she's not afraid to use it.

So unfasten your seat belt, and get ready to fly face-first through the windshield of fun! It's LIKE REAL, baby! WOOOOOOO!!!

Yer pal in the trenches,
Skipp
Portland, OR
12/30/2022

1.
A DATE WITH VIC MOSS

BOTH VIC MOSS and his reflection in the bathroom mirror regarded the other with bedroom eyes. Both spoke: "You are Harry fuckin' Styles, master of all your crafts. No woman resists you." One face beamed with hope. The other began to sweat. "You are Rocky fuckin' IV. You can hurl a log." Both voices cracked on "log."

Vic Moss closed his eyes. An aftershock of pain rippled across his face. He dry-swallowed three Tylenols and rolled his shoulders. Now, on to the business of smoothing styling goo into his lion's mane of hair, which showed no signs of recession at age 30, he was proud to note. The hair was an act of God, a wonder of the world, a perfect muff trap of thickness, silk, and the occasional chaos of a coiffed cowlick. Shabam! He felt the lightning inside. And something else. But mostly lightning. Ready to electrify.

He tilted his head side to side until a wave fell from the ranks to drape itself across his eye—peekaboo!

"You are Elvis fuckin' Presley; someone's sucking your pizzle and someone else is cooking you a rib dinner."

Three staccato yips drew his attention to Number One, his ugly little mutt pacing in the doorway.

"I won't really say that to her, Number One."

Her. *Ahh.*

Vic's was a long game with several ladies that eventually whittled down to one. It began with target acquisition. There was the woman who smiled back at him at an improv show with whom he then befriended on a single social media platform while also following her under a fake identity on another, thus gathering intel to tailor his comments. He was a fun guy, see? A guy with similar and/or complementary interests. A guy you'd want to date. When the opportunity arose, he'd send a private message for said date. Three out of four might reject the advance and/or block him. Vic would then shift attention to the fourth. Historically, he'd had a pretty good batting average with fours, and tonight a number four—who'd been his first choice in terms of desire—had agreed to meet him for dinner.

Vic congratulated himself for his persistence in the face of her many obstacles. Contact took longer than usual, and she hadn't responded to any of his cats-in-boxes memes. Most vexing, though, was the "Bring on the Meat" caption on a picture she posted of herself and an unidentified male at a summer barbecue. It irked him. All these months of steady getting-to-know-you efforts, and then, who was this guy? Why wasn't he tagged? Did she plan the double entendre? Or did she just enjoy steak?

Number One skittered out of the way as Vic half-closed the door to get the whole picture in the full-length mirror. The Vic-ture. Combined, the jeans, suit jacket and vintage Dwight Yoakam t-shirt ensemble said, "I cruise for quirky chicks at the Farmer's Market." His ashen pallor portended trouble ahead.

"Hey, Tanya, Tanya Lazonga. Ms. Lazonga. Tanya Lazonga Moss. Tanya Moss. Vic and Tanya. I'm gonna get onya, Tanya."

Number One barked again, brown eyes fixed on a pus gob leaching out of one of the several Band-Aids bedazzling the grayish, puffy landscape of Vic's right hand. Vic heedlessly grabbed a bottle of Eternity by Calvin Klein for a quick squirt-squirt into the air above him. He closed his eyes again as the sandalwood pheromones misted down upon his head and shoulders.

LIKE REAL

***

A woman's lips—a luscious creature in constant motion, slathered in lip gloss that reflected the candlelight—parted in a smile, then wrapped themselves around a straw. SLURP. A drop of vodka beaded on her pouty lower lip. She said something Vic couldn't hear over his own thick, labored breathing.

The restaurant was a mishmash of style, with gypsy violins, mid-century vinyl booths, and the co-mingling smells of basting meat, garlic and various perfumes of couples having a big night out. Might be an Italian place, what with the parmesan bottles on the tables. Servers shouldered trays of ribs hurried past the large wagon wheel on one wall and under oil paintings of Greek Gods on the other, further confounding easy classification. Was it a romance and rib dinners joint? Upscale Applebee's?

A busboy, stuffed into a ruffled Harlequin shirt and jodhpurs, prowled the dining room with his water pitcher, passing the booth where Vic sat across from the lady with the lips, aka Tanya, a 30-something cupcake in a look-at-my-tits dress and a swirly up-do smooth as chocolate Dole whip.

According to Vic's research, Tanya enjoyed traveling and yoga, Exotica music and vintage tapestry. She wrote clickbait news articles and read fantasy-noir novels, which he hadn't known was even a thing, but apparently, in certain literary circles, Mike Hammer and Sam Spade can be detectives *and* faeries. Or fight faeries. Or fuck them.

Vic's ailing right hand stayed hidden under the tablecloth.

"Um, hello? Was this in Baghdad?" She'd asked this twice, hadn't she?

He used Kenjutsu Power to refocus and re-ground himself in his surroundings. He was seated in a booth. Before they sat down, he'd half-hugged her. She smelled sweet as frosting, *mmm*, and didn't appear to notice that he kept his right hand tucked into his jacket pocket.

3

"Where was this?" She knocked on the checkered tablecloth.

"24 clicks out from Baghdad. 118 degrees Fahrenheit. More than 140 inside my gear. On my knees, with an AK-47 pointed directly at my temple. At that range it would blow a hole through me the size of your"—eyes briefly on her cleavage—"head. I had no doubt in my mind that I was going to die right then and—"

The busboy interrupted to refill water and mouth-breathe while checking out the tattoo on Tanya's shoulder: a cursive "NAMASTE" under colorful hibiscus flowers.

Tanya smiled up at him. "Will you ask our server to bring another Chi Chi?" To Vic, "Do you want another Chi Chi?"

"Yeah, I'll take a Chi Chi." The busboy nodded and toddled off. Tanya knocked on the table again. "So? You were going to die?"

"Right. I could have just lowered my head and let it happen, but I thought 'I'm going out a hero, I'm going while there's still courage in my'"—a sliver of ice trilled up to his shoulder—"'*heart!*'"

Tanya's eyes glittered with suspicion, but Vic didn't notice, heading as he was for the big story climax. "So I did that thing where you look behind someone like 'hey there's something terrible behind you!' and in the second it took him to figure out I was BS-ing him, I'd slashed his shins open with my Swiss Army knife." Her only response was a cocked eyebrow. Still, Vic pulled the chain out of his Yoakam t-shirt to show her the red dangling knife hanging next to his dog tag. "I'm also a kendoka."

"And that is?"

"I practice Kendo sword fighting."

"What a story."

"I still dream about it."

She loudly sucked the remnants of her Chi Chi, then said, "My mom used to sleep with a lot of veterans in the nineties, and this one guy had such awful nightmares that

4

one time she woke up and he was choking her. It's not like that, is it?"

"No ma'am, I whimper occasionally . . . in a very attractive way."

"Ma'am?"

The server arrived with the third round of drinks. Vic swallowed another Tylenol, chasing it with a straw full of Chi Chi. It was go-time on the *How to Win Friends & Influence People* methods. "So, you're a teacher *and* a writer? That's impressive."

Tanya wanted to take pride in herself as a writer, but the seeds of her labor often bore tasteless fruit. "I write entertainment articles, like, '10 Hairiest Chainsaw Mishaps?' Or those personality tests such as 'What Fantasy Dude are You?'"

"Jon Snow."

"Of course you are."

"He's a classic."

"Yes. I also teach Kundalini Yoga."

"I Kunda-like-that."

Tanya kinda loathed his lame pun, and the way his glassy eyes probed for contact.

"Tanya Lasagna," he said in a sing-song voice.

"Lazonga," she corrected him, as she had many others.

"Did kids used to call you Tanya Lasagna?"

"No," she lied.

Vic pointed to himself, almost proudly. "Vic the Tick. Victoria. Vicky. Dick. Dick Loss. Shit Floss. Dick Sauce. The semester I was fat it was Vic Moose or"—to combat the tornado of pain funneling up his arm, he slammed the problem hand on the booth, shouting— "*Hoss*!"

The restaurant quieted at once.

"What's going on down there?" Tanya's eyes affixed to his right arm, with the hand below deck, flopping around in throes of pain. "Did you bring a ferret or something?"

Vic slid out of the booth, keeping his hand tucked

inside his jacket a la Napoleon Bonaparte. "Bad paper cut!" he croaked, then tore off to the bathroom.

He flew past the busboy at a urinal and banged into the stall, where he raised the mysterious right hand, a disheveled mummy wrapped in paper towels and duct tape.

The busboy bounced on the balls of his feet, goaded his stream to end. It was hard to ignore the grunting in the stall.

Vic cut at the duct tape with his Swiss Army knife, then unwound it with the left hand, wincing at every movement, drawing closer to his own personal horror show. He sniffed the air. The scent of raw chicken a day past the sell date. "Uh oh."

The busboy zipped up the jodhpurs and tiptoed to the sink a chorus of "Oh no, oh no, oh noooos!" A wad of bloody duct tape rolled out from under the door, stopping him dead in his tracks. Then, despite his better judgement, he leaned in towards the stall . . .

Meanwhile, Vic's pupils dilated as he peeled off the last paper towel, wincing as the final bits stuck to the crust on his flesh. "*God. GOD!*"

Whatever the busboy spied between crack and door shot him back like a grenade blast. He ignored the *employees: wash your hands* sign as he raced out of the bathroom.

Back at the booth, Tanya watched the busboy cross the dining room. If this wasn't a restaurant, she'd swear he was a Ren Faire actor OD-ing on gummies.

***

Tanya nudged open the bathroom door with her foot. She kept her eyes closed. "Hello? Vic?"

Bloody paper towels swirled down the toilet bowl. Vic, face wet and pale, wrapped his suit jacket around the hand. "Tanya?"

"Everything okay?"

"Yep. Be out in two shakes of a very big stick."

LIKE REAL

Tanya opened her eyes to roll them, then ducked out.

When he heard the door snick shut, Vic swiped his cell active with his nose and screamed at it: "Okay, Google, call Norman!"

***

"Why does it stink so much? Whhhhhyyyyy?"

Norman, a friendly chap wearing a Members Only jacket and a Willie Nelson braid, squinted at his buddy in the rearview mirror. He was curled in a fetal position in the back seat, head abutting the baby seat. Probably the worst employee he'd ever managed, but one of his best friends. He'd considered himself the maker of good employees and still hadn't given up on Pygmalion-ing Vic into a responsible and thoughtful worker bee. Plus, he made a solid wingman at karaoke bars to Norman's middle-aged, divorced, ruined ass. "Are we talking about the baby seat? Or are we talking about—"

"Meeeeee!" Vic screamed. "About meeee!"

"Best not to speculate."

The Subaru screeched to a halt at the ER entrance. Automatic doors whirred open and Norman half-dragged Vic inside.

"Somebody's gotta save this guy's hand, stat!"

The admitting nurse glanced up from her phone, blanching as Vic and Norman staggered to her station.

"My hand!" Vic wailed, brandishing a gray, bloated blob with sausage fingers and volcano calderas percolating with ooze.

2.
ALL I GOT WAS BLOOD CRUST

TANYA SAW HERSELF as if from an aerial camera hovering at the level of the ceiling where a mural of Italy served as a reminder that this was an Italian restaurant. She and Vic had laughed about the incongruent design motif. Well, she had. Vic nodded and chortled as if he didn't understand English.

She lowered her head to suck the third Chi Chi to its end. Her cleavage sparkled with glittery body lotion, and her dress was something a Russ Meyer starlet might wear to a cocktail party. But the hour-and-a-half of intense stylization had evidently come to die here in this vinyl booth, where she waited for her date to emerge from the bathroom.

When Vic turned into a deranged Muppet, screaming, "Hoss," and bouncing out of the booth to skip-run to the bathroom, every single person in the restaurant took note. And, though he'd been gone at least five minutes, the patrons remained vigilant, dividing their attention between the bathroom area and Tanya, who waited alone in the booth.

What a waste of time. She mentally flogged herself for not detecting the signs. First contact had been a picture of Vic with his adorable bedhead and his ugly little dog. He held a computer-related job and practiced Japanese sword fighting. On one hand, he might be considered upwardly mobile, athletic and disciplined. On the other, he could be a Dahmer. But those types usually slipped, dropping an Easter Egg in a late-night post that set everyone's arm hairs on fire.

But Vic behaved perfectly, validating most of her posts with an emoji or a comment and tagging her on cute memes. His responses hinted but did not broach outright flirtation. Intoxicated by the attention, she found herself drifting into first-kiss, first-dance, first-fuck fantasies.

Except, as time drew on, she noticed all the various social media surveys he shared cast him as Jon Snow, Romeo, that Witcher dude, Daryl from *Walking Dead*, Paris, Cake, and Least Likely to Die in a Zombie Apocalypse, which made her laugh because she wrote it. Such a proud moment for her family to see her byline under a picture of a zombie hag slurping intestines out of a dead guy's gut.

She'd lifted many questions from an old Cold War-era book about psychopaths and sociopaths; he picked at least four out of ten answers labeled as sociopathic, hence survival in the event of an apocalypse. The final clue, and what should prevented this a date altogether, involved a travel poll titled "What is your Dream Vacation?" His initial result was Thailand. But two weeks later, it changed to Greece. Boom! Slip-up. He was herding her into a kill pen by publishing polls with results complementing the few polls she chose to show the world. She was Daenerys, "before she got ridiculously homicidal" and Paris was the city in which she should live. If she were a dessert, she'd be ice cream to his cake. And Greece was her dream vacation.

"There's your slip-up, dummy," she'd said to her phone in regard to his new dream vacation. "Thailand was fine, it wasn't a deal breaker. You got obvious." But where alarm bells might have rung for other gals, Tanya went deaf, and agreed to meet for dinner.

She waited five minutes before checking on him. He'd

be out in "two shakes of a very big stick." What a cartoonish Lothario, blurring the line between ironic and idiotic. Vowing to remember that phrasing to write about later, she signaled the server for the check, then attacked the dregs of her Chi Chi.

How do I extricate from this mess, she wondered, and received her answer when Vic emerged from the bathroom, face like actual snow, not Jon Snow. The arm he'd kept hidden was now wrapped in his jacket. He shambled across the dining room, bumped into a stack of booster seats, then somehow veered close enough to the booth to say, "I've got a minor emergency." His tongue struggled to articulate words. "Do-over?"

Before she had a chance to respond, he bolted. Nobody in the restaurant tried to conceal their rubbernecking as he lurched out the front door. Busby Berkeley would have admired the subsequent wave of heads swiveling back for her reaction.

The check billfold appeared in a manicured hand. Dean Martin finally finished "That's Amore" which, as per usual, would stick in her head for days. She dug out a credit card and flopped it down, then fixated on the red lava candle, listening with relief as the crowd resumed their conversations.

When the server returned, Tanya wrote in a huge tip, grabbed her boho shawl and quilted clutch, and exited the booth with the dignity of a woman so committed to namaste and its loop of bliss she had it tattooed on her shoulder.

As she passed Vic's side of the booth, her heel caught something. She felt it immediately. Impaled on her spiky heel was a paper towel stained with a dollop of blood. Now she had her angle. Her next MyDiary entry would be titled "All I Got From this Date Was Blood Crust."

3.
VIC'S LOSS

SOMEHOW, NORMAN HAD disappeared from Vic's side, and Vic found himself in a fluorescent artery of the ER that smelled like a piss martini. Around him were bustling paramedics, a child's wailing, the beeping of machines. And above it all, the pulsing pain in his hand.

Two orderlies—a lanky tatted gent, and a bullet-shaped wrestler type—grappled him towards a gurney. After some wailing and kicking, Vic dead-weighted them until he broke through their fingers.

The molasses-slow trip to the floor allowed him a pocket of time to consider if he'd ever felt this type of pain before. Maybe the night his dad punched him in the gut, which had been fortuitous since the doctors discovered appendicitis and then sent him to live with Paps.

When Vic finally thumped to the laminate floor, the orderlies pounced, twisting him up like a rodeo calf. An RN jabbed a needle in his arm. "These are the kind of nights that make you want to drink all day," he said, sitting back on his heels, ready for a micro nap.

The trio watched Vic's transformation. Nobody blinked. "And away he goes," said the shorter orderly. Vic's feeble whimpering had ceased, and he looked around as if waking up from a nice nap.

"Norman's taking care of Number One," he assured everyone. Then, with an orderly's hand under each armpit, allowed himself to be eased onto the awaiting gurney. "Am I gonna die?"

"No, dude," replied the bigger orderly. "But it ain't gonna be pretty." *The dragon tattoo on his neck is pretty sweet*, Vic thought as the gurney began to move.

"He *probably* won't die," corrected the doctor, who joined alongside. Vic squinted up at her . . . the name tag said Doctor Suki. *Hmmm. Beautiful, middle-aged, still tight.* She could definitely play a doctor in the Canadian softcore porn he loved so much. Another thought: If he died, his porn would disturb absolutely no one. What a pity.

"Mr. Moss, can you tell me what happened?" Doctor Suki asked.

Instead of an answer, he sang: "Lady doctor, she's a lady. Doctor Suki, gonna save me . . . "

"All right, to the point. Have you recently seen spiders in your home?"

Spiders, plural. Not mosquitos. *Of course spiders*, he thought. The boils went south so fast. He should have gone to Urgent Care. The minute those bumps developed a patina, he shoulda. But when Vic Moss makes a date with a gal . . .

"The bite of the brown recluse is more dangerous than a black widow's. And they're having a population boom, thanks to the drought."

The numbness rendering Vic into a happy idiot now became a palette for questionable memories of terrible events, so when the doc told him "they can nest in trees," Vic pictured his bedroom window, and the tree branches tickling its glass. A perfect spider bridge!

She continued, "They live in attics, in boxes, in cupboards, in walls, in shoes even."

Vic saw a brown spider scuttle towards his bed, to the lip of the comforter dusting the floor. From there, an easy hike up to the mattress.

"As with roaches, if you see a single recluse, you can bet there are many more in the vicinity."

The orderlies exchanged a look. Doctor Suki loved delivering all the scary details, which was why they nicknamed her "Doctor Spooky."

"The good news is, they are not social creatures, hence the name 'recluse.' So if they're in your house, it's somewhere quiet and dark, and they will not attack, unless disturbed."

Vic mulled whether the image of himself using a shoe to smash a spider creeping up his bedroom wall was real or imagined.

"Their bite is quite venomous, let alone three . . . "

Vic watched his own self sleeping in bed, on his side. His right hand, lolling off the edge of the mattress, teemed with spiders.

" . . . and if left untreated, well . . . " Her sweeping hand gesture summed up Vic's predicament.

***

Vic was king of the parade. Royal attendants wheeled his throne past his all his subjects—nurses, doctors, patients, hooray! An administrator trotting alongside got his Hancock on forms. The throne picked up speed; lights soared above him in endless shooting stars.

His brief reign ended when a few scary words in the orderlies' conversation wormed into his ear: " . . . blah, blah, blah, gangrene . . . blah, blah-blah . . . necrosis . . . blah-blah-blah . . . amputation."

The gurney pounded through the operating room doors.

***

The following day, Vic sat slumped in a wheelchair at the hospital's pickup curb. A Mylar Get-Well balloon was tied around his good wrist. His glazed eyes lingered on his right arm, which tapered into a bandaged stump with the thumb poking out. A horrible plaster cocoon and a lonely thumb. Despite the hospital drugs, he still felt the ache in a hand that no longer existed.

This is all gonna be part of a good story someday, he

told himself. *Maybe over a romantic make-up dinner with Tanya. We'll laugh and laugh and then we'll do it.*

***

Norman, inexplicably wearing a denim 1970s Billy Joel hat, pulled the seat belt across Vic's chest and snapped him in. On their brief journey, Vic detected the scent of the carnitas burrito Norman ate for lunch but digested none of his platitudes about "clean slates," "new dawns," or "the road ahead," which, "though littered with obstacles," would strengthen his character.

Instead, Vic tried to puzzle together bits of an idea on how he'd rebuild his life and not put things off anymore. He'd go to the doctor and stop with the endless social media quizzes he took repeatedly to simpatico himself with some cutie-pie he worked like a mark.

He'd start using the *Killing It 110% and Beyond* app he'd been developing since last year, free himself from the yoke of mindless programming for someone else's financial gain and make it right with Tanya. Yeah. So what if the first date was disastrous? "Everyone starts at zero," Norman would say. Or "things can only get better from here." The key was to set the bar low, then do a high jump.

A series of billboards caught his eye as Norman drove them into the northeast valley. Lap Bands programmed and regulated by computers. Plastic surgery services that didn't leave you with a strange puppet face. And a new prostheses people could control with their minds.

"Home again, home again, jiggity-jig." Norman steered the Subaru to the curb outside Vic's apartment complex. Vic gaped at him helplessly. "You can do it," Norman said. "First step is the seat belt."

Vic un-belted himself. "Thanks, Norman, for everything."

"Once upon a time, I got kicked to the curb, and you picked me up and put me on your couch for two months. This is just one notch on a much longer checklist."

Vic nodded, eyes welling up. He loved Norman.

"Now get out and go make yourself better, stronger, faster."

Vic shoved the plastic hospital bag filled with his belongings under his right armpit. They still reeked of cologne from date night.

Norman's brow furrowed as Vic wrangled the balloon out of the back seat and then tottered to the security gate, shouldering it till it squeaked open. Norman slipped a little notebook and pen out of his shirt pocket and wrote *gate needs WD-40!!! By the* time he looked up, Vic was inside. He double-honked a goodbye and pulled away from the curb. *Time for some Marianne Williamson*, he thought, reaching for his stereo.

***

Vic heard dance pop coming from the pool area while he lingered by the cluster of mailboxes as though checking his mail. *Why couldn't it be a little scar on the cheek instead? That would play so much better than the world's saddest one-handed Romeo, that's for sure.* He could delay no longer, so made his way into the complex proper, where two stories of apartments wrapped around a kidney-shaped pool. Manicured shrubs and mini palm and lemon trees encircled the strip of concrete bordering the pool, and the little patio with plastic chairs and tables.

The chief attraction: two middle-aged Barbies in bikinis on reclining loungers. Sun rays bounced off the pool to dance across their taut, leathery torsos. One Barbie's name was Cozy, short for Cozetta, and her sister was Mamie, short for god knows what. Unless you looked closely, you couldn't tell them apart.

He dawdled at the stairs, waiting for the sisters to notice him, enjoying the smell of their cocoa-buttered bodies. They sat up in tandem and waved. Vic waved back, "accidentally" letting go of the balloon. A meek grab for the string, but with his right hand—old habits!—and thumb couldn't do it alone, so away it drifted . . . up . . . up . . . first floor, second floor, sky, goodbye!

Mamie said, "Aw, noooo."

Cozy said, "The balloon, aw."

And then they both said, sort of as an echo of the other, "Vic lost his balloon."

Somewhere violins swelled as Vic lumbered upstairs. He wasn't above pity in the absence of pussy.

His place overlooked the deep end of the pool, and he'd often talked himself out of cannonballing over the railing during one of the Barbies' legendary pool parties. He wrestled with the key, pitying the upcoming learning curve his left hand had yet to endure.

The design aesthetic of his apartment was third-hand junk with a Japanese vibe. He found the couch on a curb. It was in perfect condition, though purple and velvet. An antique wooden shipping trunk functioned as the coffee table. It had traveled with his great-grandfather from Japan to many ports of the world and was once loaded with bibles and burlap sacks of dried food and clothing. Great-grandfather successfully converted an Okinawa woman to Presbyterianism, then married her. Her dowry included paintings, which is how Vic acquired the several oil renderings of Japanese life in the late 19th century, titled "Lovers in a Garden," "A Boy and his Dog," and "Birds and Maidens."

His prize painting depicted a perilous journey of the 18th-century Japanese frigate and warship, the Hoo Maru, captured on canvas with its black-banded sails and the lacquered bow cutting through the crest of a wave. The ship's near 45-degree angle revealed the copper sheathing that came up to the water line. Behind the ship, a horizon roiled with storm clouds. This painting was always in his life, in his grandparents' home. Some nights, Vic dreamed he stood at the bow of the Hoo Maru, peering through binoculars at a far-away shore but never got any closer to it.

If the Hoo Maru was his prized painting, the swords were his most cherished possessions, after Number One of course. Two wooden practice bokutos rested on mounts above and below the mount holding his real steel-bladed katana. Vic ran his lonely thumb down its shaft to the handle. Would he ever practice Kendo again?

He wandered over to his bistro table where his little mutt, Number One, was curled up on a chair. The little fellow yawned, then rolled onto his back. "Too tired to come to the door, Number One? You didn't miss me?" Vic reached for his belly. "Who's my happy boy? Who's my little baby boo-boo? Unfortunately, he used the wrong hand, freaking out the dog, who bared his teeth and growled." Number One bared his teeth. "I know, it's upsetting. It's all gone, Number One, but I still got my thumb." Number One scampered into the living room, growling. "Aw, don't be that way."

Later, Vic pushed away sad thoughts so he could begin acclimating to using his subordinate hand. It awkwardly wielded a Sharpie to write "Victor Moss" on the inside of an empty pizza box, over and over, but the cursive never got more sophisticated than the signature of a five-year-old.

"Loss is a part of life. Life ends in loss. The ultimate loss," Vic quoted Norman who'd told him he was paraphrasing himself. It was both confusing and sad. Now, he couldn't single-handedly pop the top off his child-proof prescription bottle. *Who the fuck am I talking to?* he thought. The battle against self-pity was a tough one, especially in moments where he found his thumb completely useless. "What is your function?!" he shouted at his right thumb. "Fuck this." He used the left hand and his teeth.

"Vic-tory." He dropped two pills on his tongue, thinking how "Vic-tory" would have been a good addition to the litany of nicknames he'd revealed to Tanya. Except the only person who ever called him "Vic-tory" was himself.

He marched into the living room, ignoring Number

17

One's accusatory glare, and grabbed a bokuto. He rotated it in a circle-eight to warm up his wrist, then began a series of combat poses. But his game was shot, if he ever had any with the left hand, which was never alpha, and therefore had no muscle memory of the routines.

"You're weak," he hollered at his left hand, before moving into an awkward turn-and-thrust that situated him in direct view of his bedroom door. This was the first time he balls-out looked at it since returning from the hospital.

That door used to be the entryway to his sacred resting and humping chamber. Now it was the portal to spider town. Every thought in his head involved walking away, backing up, turning around. Avoid whatever's in there because it was probably scary.

Nay, Vic decided, stalking to the bedroom with his bokuto. *I'm going out a hero, I'm going out while there's still courage in my heart.* He tucked the sword under his arm, turned the knob, inched it open, stuck his head in, eyes darting from corners to the space under the bed, to the window, which was thankfully closed. With no spiders sighted, his head glided out and he shut the door. A good first step.

Later, Vic used his left hand and teeth to tear off a long strip of duct tape. Number One watched from a safe distance. Vic smoothed the tape over the crack between door and door frame, beginning at the top.

***

Outside, the sun dropped behind the building. Tiki torches flared to life. More Barbies and some Kens assembled around the pool.

Upstairs, Vic surfed a dating site he knew Tanya frequented. Women's images reflected off his computer glasses as he scrolled. He'd used a fake name and an AI-augmented photo, so he'd have access to her particulars without her knowing it was him. God forbid she ever reached out to chadinthevalley.

On the TV, a horny housewife and a lady plumber met

in a kitchen with a leaky faucet. "Well, I'll be flummoxed. A female plumber, eh? You don't see that every day."

"I get the job done better than any male plumber, I can promise that, ma'am," replied the husky-voice plumbette. "I can do A to Zed and letters you've not heard of before."

Vic found Tanya, enlarged her photo to full screen.

"My husband is a plumber, but this isn't a job for him . . . "

Vic sighed, shut the laptop. And, despite the plumber and the housewife being now topless and writhing around on the open door of the dishwasher, he switched off the TV to investigate the splashing and laughing outside. He drifted over to his venetian blinds like a floating Dracula, tried to open the blinds with his stump. He sighed, switching hands.

The Barbies dunked each other in the shallow end. Vic saw no others, having eyes only for the life vest Cozy wore over her bikini. In theory, it should irritate him to be denied cleavage, but he rather enjoyed the mystery of a polyethylene chastity belt. *Do you dig through it?* he wondered. *Hell yeah! You got two thumbs, Vic the quick, Vic with the mighty dick!*

His stump crept down his torso to his tummy to his zipper, forgetting, reaching, then alas, remembering the lost fingers. The blinds snapped shut, and Vic wept for his great loss.

4.
LIKEREAL.NET

VIC PURSED HIS lips as he beheld his computer screen, which displayed the beta version of *Killing It 110% and Beyond*. He knew the title was hyperbolic, but the target audience would be true believers, buying any product featuring an image or marketing language evoking a predator beast. After they did their reps and drank their HGH milkshakes, they'd want to log it for posterity, then use that data as a baseline goal to demolish the next day.

Under Daily Goals he typed: *how to repair most of your damage.*

Even if a guy doesn't believe the words coming to mind or mouth—say if he's mantra-ing the phrase "I will find goodness in this day" but knows in his heart he'll spend the day compiling a litany of complaints to brood upon until slumber arrives via a sleep aid and *Family Feud*—if he keeps at it, eventually he'll believe. All he needs is muscle memory. Similarly, with training, Vic's left hand might do more than hold his balls.

At some point while Vic was picturing his balls, the painkillers kicked in, his eyes lost focus, and he dropped sideways onto the couch until his head landed on his Japanese neck pillow. The last rays of the sun through the blinds noir-striped his face in amber shadows.

***

Suns set, suns rose, doggie took walks, Vic put on pants, but didn't shave or shower. He had too much acclimating to do and found himself constantly disappointed by his left hand for many reasons, but primarily because the lethal combination of its ineptitude and his desperation prompted a few over-the-clothes relations with his couch. Number One's silent observation also threw a freak blanket over everything. The unblinking black eyes bored into his back, forcing hard questions, such as: *if I cum while the dog is watching, does that mean I get off on the dog watching?*

***

Saturday morning. Sounds of a classic K-Pop girl-group drifted from poolside to outside the security gate, where Norman was busy applying WD-40 to its hinges. He bobbed his head along to Black Pink's "Boombayah," about a bad girl who doesn't want a boy, she wants a man.

When they say "man," they mean a 32-year-old, tops. Many guys his age got that wrong and made asses of themselves or got put on lists. Norman knew his place, even in idle fantasies while handyman-ing. He pocketed the WD-40, picked up the meats-cookies-pickles gift basket by his feet and entered. The gate no longer squeaked but the sumabitch still stuck a little.

He reduced his speed so's to enjoy the sight of the bikini-attired Barbies setting up their deck chairs.

In turn, they spotted him loitering at the foot of the stairs. Ponytail, gift basket, shorts with a windbreaker . . . feh.

Norman waved with his free hand. "I spy early birds catching the first rays."

The sisters exchanged a glance; Mamie would deal with this guy. "Yep. It's gonna be a scorcher."

"In September. Almost autumn."

"Uh-huh."

"I fixed the squeak on the gate, but the frame is bent."

"Thank you. We'll tell our guy."

"I'm stronger than I look, but that bugger requires Hercules."

Chuckling insincerely, the sisters unfurled their spa towels with simultaneous snaps.

Norman smelled dismissal under the coconut body oil. Hell's bells, they were in his appropriate age range. *Who do they think they're kidding?* He'd flailed his way through a hurricane of betrayal and divorce and rejection and considered himself immune to their painful surges. But it aggravated him.

"Have a great day, ma'am, ma'am."

He waited for their reaction—did their shoulders stiffen?—then went upstairs, spindly legs taking two at a time.

Four knocks until the door opened and there stood before him, shirtless in sweatpants, the stinky hippy formerly known as Vic Moss, Junior Programmer.

What's sadder, Norman mused as he cleared a space on the couch, *the wispy beard? Or the Cheeto finger stains on the pants?* He swatted judgement from his mind and got to the business of spreading dozens of brochures and flyers over empty pizza boxes.

"I know I look bad," Vic said, pawing through the basket.

"But you smell sublime."

"I'll clean up when I go back to work."

"And when is that?"

"Two weeks from Monday." Vic found a jar of dill pickles. Hooray!

"Wonderful. It's busy."

Vic tapped the jar's lid against the coffee trunk to loosen it. "Did we get our stock options yet?"

"We got promising talks." Norman held up a flyer. "Check it."

"'Healing Begins Within?' No shit, Stormin' Norman. How 'bout a one-handed typing class?"

Norman found another. "Here's a thing, you enjoy karaoke."

"Chicks in wheelchairs singing 'I Will Survive?' Next."

Norman dropped the flyer with a dad-sized sigh. Vic tried handing off the pickles, but Norman was all about life lessons right now.

"Here's what I tell my baby girl and will now tell you: Life isn't fair and nobody's perfect." His eyes drifted off into a memory. "She didn't take it well, but someday, she and you will acknowledge its depth and clarity. For cryin' out loud, it's the key to contentment."

"Does that mean you won't help me?" Vic nodded to the jar.

"Buddy, if you can do that with one hand"—Vic followed his glance to the bedroom door, which was closed, with layers of duct tape sealing its perimeters—"you can sure as hell open a jar of pickles."

A good mentee, Vic considered this a validation, and it gave him strength. Using his knees and his left hand, he twisted the lid until it popped, and then he popped a dill into his maw, chewing triumphantly.

Norman selected a rectangular door-knob flyer. "Found this sucker on your gate, which no longer squeaks, thanks to this guy."

Vic abandoned the pickles, eyes glued to the flyer, colored sky blue, with a cartoon foot hovering in mid-air, a hand growing out the top of the foot and an eyeball on the ankle. Strident font at the bottom advertised: *likereal.net*

Five pickles later, Norman bid him adieu. His last words at the door were: "'Belief is powerful, and whatever we believe, we will subconsciously make manifest.' Marianne Williamson."

"All right, thanks, man," Vic replied after pausing long enough so Norman would think he got a nugget of wisdom from the words. Vic admired Norman's capacity for pulling out memorized quotes for every occasion, although it irritated him every single time.

"Where're my . . . " Norman glanced around the room,

then touched his sunglasses, propped up on his head. "Ha!" A last finger point at Vic, "Belief, Vic, belief," and he left.

Vic stared at the flyer.

***

The address bar read: likereal.net. Below, the disembodied foot/hand/eyeball revolved in slow flash animation as site buttons took their sweet ass time materializing. Tinny 8-bit music played a synthesized classical ditty, no doubt meant to sound inspirational. Vic felt it'd be more appropriate as the ironic music you play before you kill yourself in a motel room in Norwalk.

Before & After photos materialized slow as developing Polaroids.

"Fucking amateurs," Vic mumbled. "Is this 1995?"

First up: "Peter." In his thirties. The Before photo showed him in a wheelchair, one leg ending at the knee. In the After shot, the wheelchair had disappeared, and Peter was squatting to hug a dog. The shorts he wore showed off two identical, realistic legs.

Next up: "Sgt. Joan." The Before photo depicted a female Army Sergeant with two empty uniform sleeves. Vic shook his head, pained, not just because she was a fellow service person, but because she probably lost her arms in combat. Meanwhile, Vic pretended the big red bumps on his hand were results of a heretofore unknown allergy, maybe too much gluten, or the puritan god's way of shaming his self-love avocation—anything but the death bites of brown recluses that had somehow gotten into his bed.

The After photo showed her in a short-sleeved Mrs. Claus costume, handing a gift to a little boy. Two arms. Two hands. Big smile. He enlarged the screen. The details looked so real, with nails and freckles even. The boy's face bothered him, though. Somber eyes.

Was this all real? As a computer scientist, Vic's first instinct was always pragmatic skepticism. However, judging by the overall shittiness of the site, he doubted anyone involved had intermediate-or-beyond Photoshop skills, which meant it might be real.

Finally, there was "Hank," a man bearing one eye, and an empty socket. The After picture was identical, except for a question mark over the eye socket, and the words *Coming Soon*.

A beach ball spun, and a pop-up loaded next to Hank's question mark. Giant font announced: *See Hank live, TONIGHT! "You Can Overcome!"*

Vic turned to Number One, who was busy licking his junk at the far end of the couch. "I don't know about you, Number One, but one can never over-cum . . . amiright?"

Number One looked up, tongue lolling through the gap in his icky little teeth.

5.

THE LONE THUMBMAN

HER TAT WAS the kind popular with white girls, normally as a tramp stamp on their lower back, but this reporter, with her librarian glasses and sensible shoes, wore the tat on her bare shoulder, and, even better, wore shirts that emphasized her dulces hermanas. The lanky orderly, aka Eddie, admired her for these contradictions, and for the giant plate of cookies she always brought with her when she came seeking the scoop, as she called it.

Two days ago, he got her texts, which were more of a short story broken into six non-sequential stanzas that took him half his break to puzzle together.

Assembled, it read:

Hey Eddie, it's Tanya. I scoured crime blotters & live incident feeds from last weekend, Sat night after 9 pm. The person would not have used an ambulance & no police report yet. I know something happened b/c I was there when the crisis began, approx 8p Sat. I wrote about the event. The lady is obviously me but fictionalized and embellished. Go to https://tanyalazzongastories. mydiary.com/ the access password is readtanyawrite. Jeesh, srry, being freelance means I'm always in promote mode! I know u work swing shift on sats so hoping u can help. This would be a guy around 30 with probs with his arm or hand. if u did, r u avail to meet in the usual spot?

LIKE REAL

Remember I pay for pics. Hope u got pics. As usual, u r 'a hospital source' LMK ASAP. TU TL.

Being her inside source in the ER was a perk of the job Eddie hadn't expected. His was a constant struggle to not pout about how nurses made ten times his salary and to remember that he got medical and dental for himself and his kid. He even stayed married to the old lady so she could stay covered. The 90 per paycheck deductible was well worth it to keep that moody bruja off his ass. So, yeah, the occasional cookies and eye candy were much appreciated.

To his friends, he'd always referred to her as Deep Throat, because when she needed some ghastly detail, she'd text him from an unlisted number, but identify herself up top—more of her contradictions—and then they'd meet by the trash cans in the upper parking lot. From there, he'd recount ER penny dreadfuls to her.

After a recent *X-Files* binge, Eddie realized that all these months he'd been calling her by the wrong nickname. If the Cigarette Smoking Man was Deep Throat, that would make her Fox Mulder, and himself Deep Throat. And no way was he going to call himself that. He fancied himself more the handsome Lone Gunman to her Scully.

Eddie exited the parking elevator, rubber gloves tucked into the back pockets of his scrubs swatting his ass as he strutted over to the trash bins, where Scully paced. The plate of cookies she was holding landed firmly in his crosshairs.

They gave each other a conspiratorial nod and strolled over to the edge of the mostly empty lot, to the rail where they could see the backside of the hospital, and the mountains beyond.

Today, she sought deets on the dude with the spider bites. Today, she wore a tight, sleeveless cashmere sweater. And the cookies appeared to be white chocolate chip.

"Whatchugot?" she asked, gifting him with the sturdy paper plate. He tore at the saran wrap almost before she retracted her hand, then crammed a whole cookie in his mouth. His eyes rolled back with delight as he chomp-chomped.

"The cranberries, damn. Unexpected, but choice," he crooned, catching the crumbs in his hand, and licking them up.

She dug through her purse. Napkin bits, gum wrappers and pens threatened to spill over the edges, until she finally extracted her miniature notebook. Now he must earn the cookies.

"Okay, last Saturday night, after nine I think, this guy goes apeshit in the lobby. To set the scene, there's been this big late-summer flu outbreak, so there are like 40 people, half of them in masks, or wrapped in blankets, and everyone flips out cuz this guy is fighting us and shouting his hand is rotting, he's all 'my hand is fucking rotting, my haaaand!' and he was thrusting it at people. Fucking Frankenstein on PCP, know what I mean?"

She gasped and nodded. She was a good audience.

"I guess the adrenaline gave him super strength because it took both me and Curtis to get him into the O.R."

He rewarded himself with another cookie, foreseeing a nap in the supply room later once the sugar crushed him down.

"Did you see his hand?"

"Oh yeah." He plucked the cigarette off the cookie plate—her bonus gift—and took his time lighting it with old matches. He dragged until it hurt, then watched the smoke plume against the backdrop of the jagged Verdugo mountains, which at this moment were casting a shadow on his mom's house, over the mountain in Acton.

"Not only did I see it, I smelled it, and I probably touched it, but I had gloves on."

He knew she was getting impatient by the way she shifted from foot to foot, but he still made her wait while he coughed out monoxide and part of a cranberry, and then puffed on it again. Maybe he *was* the Cigarette Smoking Man.

"And . . . ?"

"So, before I got this job, me and my cousin collected recyclables. Sometimes we had to go down alleys to the dumpsters behind apartments. Okay, so one night we found a piece of pork so fucking rotted not even cats or rats would touch it. The thing had like cancer cysts or, infected blisters, and it stank worse than anything, worse than my Aunt Myrna's feet after she gets off a shift. I mean, you could taste it. That's how the dude smelled."

"Gangrene."

Eddie nodded, wondering which of his choice quotes she'd use in her article; hoping she wouldn't mention Aunt Myrna by name, because that would blow his cover.

Tanya persisted. "How? What happened to him?"

Just to mess with her, Eddie popped another cookie in his mouth, masticating fully, before saying, "Spiders."

She scrawled on her pad, eyes ablaze; a bloodhound catching the scent of putrefaction.

"Brown recluse bites. Multiple. Forget exactly, but I want to say three."

She nodded. "I'll say 'several.' Please continue."

"Okay, so I guess he let it go too long and so the surgeon . . . " Eddie used a cookie as a pretend saw cutting off his wrist.

"Amputation?"

"Partial."

"Meaning?"

"His fingers. So all he's got left is the thumb. Looks weird. I felt bad for the dude. He kept yakking about his dog. Here he was, all fucked and shit and he's worried about his dog."

"Did you get a picture?"

"Why would I take a picture?"

"For the moolah! Hello?"

"What? So you can caption the picture like, 'oh hey, look at this poor no-finger-bastard's poor dog? He used to get a full scratching, but all he gets now is a thumbing.'"

"Are you kidding?"

"Probably not. Damn these cookies are good."

"I meant a picture of *him*, the guy, or his hand. Preferably the hand."

"Well, I had *my* hands full."

"Fine, but next time, remember . . ."

They said it together: "Always take a picture."

"You mock, but I pay for pictures."

He tossed his smoke to the ground, squashing it with his rubber-sole shoe.

"I got benefits. I'm cool. But I'll try to remember for next time." He glanced at his iWatch. "Shizz. My break is done. If I'm lucky, I get to clean up old lady diarrhea tonight. Word." He folded the saran wrap over the cookies and fist-bumped her goodbye.

On his walk to the elevator, he figured out the perfect fake name for the dude, courtesy of his recent *X-Files* binge. "Hey!" He cupped his hands around his mouth. "In your story? You should call him 'The Lone Thumbman.'" She laughed. He gave her a thumbs-up and got into the elevator.

Tanya leaned against the rail, admiring reds and golds of sunset playing against the mountains. She pitied The Lone Thumbman. Did she emit a certain energy frequency that attracted problematic men like moths? Was it also coded into her DNA to half-fall in love with them while simultaneously exploiting their dilemmas for articles and MyDiary entries? *Nope*, she thought, *in return for my heart, I am thusly rewarded, it's just little ol' me making lemonade from lemons.*

She began the spiral descent down the parking structure, avoiding the elevator; and berating herself for not stockpiling cookies in her car. Once inside, she pulled out her phone and scrolled to the texts Vic sent her hours before the "Paper Towel Incident."

Vic: *Reservation at 8* (thumbs-up emoji)

Tanya: (emoji of a happy face in sunglasses)

LIKE REAL

Vic: (winky-wink emoji)

Oh, the stupid hope she'd allowed herself to feel at the prospect of meeting the guy with the ugly dog and the adorable bedhead.

She texted: *Hi, you own me*

"Stupid auto spell!" She pressed the delete key and fixed the text: *Hi, you owe me*

Her thumbs hovered indecisively. Was she overcome by sympathy? Or did common sense dictate she'd have a better chance at contact if she let him deal with some issues first? Why was she perpetually asking herself but not answering any of her own questions? Was that the key to her failure?

As she started the car, it occurred to her that according to Eddie, The Lone Thumbman still had both thumbs, meaning he could text. She took comfort in that.

6.

HANK

VIC CROSSED A ragged lawn by the light of the church's LED sign that read: *You Can Overcome 7:30.*

Warm Santa Ana winds tickled his scraggly beard and rustled the palm trees around him. As with most decisions, Vic froze at the crossroads. Not content to take a chance but rather to analyze chance versus fate. Would he go inside? Was going inside a matter of simple fate? Or a trick by God to show him he'd made the wrong decision long ago? Or was it a figment of Vic's mind, in the area where he still held onto a smidge of religious dread?

Sundays as a kid, he attended Mass, then bible study, then to his cousins' house. When the adults went outside to barbecue and drink, and the cousins took off on their bikes, Vic was left alone to creep on the family's Catholic bible, a five-pound source of delicious terror on its own wooden pedestal.

Vic absconded with the bible to a dark corner of the living room. As he flipped through its delicate pages, organ music playing in his head, he'd trace a finger over quotes written in raised gold ink and always paid visits to a few of his favorite images such as Salome holding John the Baptist's severed head on a platter.

All he knew about the story was that Princess Salome, daughter of King Herod, demanded John's head and got it, and was showing it off to the painter. Her impassive face and dark sloping eyes held no regret; the upstretched arms formed with delicate fleshy curves. Then there was the head. John's head. He was a guy once. Now he's dead. He's just a head! Where is the body? Vic was certain Salome ate the head for dinner. His guess on which part she'd eat first varied. Some Sundays, she peeled and sucked out the eyeball. Other Sundays, she dug into the cheek first. Would she get beard hair in her teeth?

He visited any depiction of Lucifer, or demons, or the archangels. And he'd finish with a bit of Revelations. To expect God's favorites to Rapture, leaving himself, other sinners and non-Christian people to fight demons, drove a cold terror from his heart down through his limbs, and he'd go hide in the hall closet until Dad found and punished him later.

He dropped religion in his second semester of college and became a hellfire and brimstone atheist. Though he calmed down with time, he retained a disdain for believers. Didn't they know the constant thoughts of dying, being dead, going to hell, or being bored to shit in heaven goes away once you stop thinking magically?

That the meet-group tonight was at a church didn't concern him. The place hosted AA, NA, ALANON, Weight Watchers, Unitarians, and self-help seminars. There would be no stained glass or tortured saints inside, no fear of religious inklings mushrooming to the levels of his hall closet days.

By his phone it was 7:47. The meeting had started, and he wasn't sure if he dared enter late. He moved closer for recon at the large front window, crouching behind the manicured hedge for a peek inside. Shadows in folding chairs listened to the speaker, a well-lit man wearing Ray Charles glasses. Must be Hank.

Vic strained to hear him.

" . . . a wounded rodent, scuttling into corners . . . letting events carry you on the wind like a leaf . . . then you are already dead."

Those tantalizing scary words, and the sighting of a table loaded with boxes of donuts, were enough to get Vic onto the long ranch-style porch running alongside the building. Tiny halogen lights lit his path as he approached the side door. On the way, he stuffed his bandaged thumb-stump into his jacket pocket.

Once inside, he let his eyes adjust. He spied at least two walkers, three wheelchairs, a dude hunched over with his head in his hands, and a twitchy feller in back.

No women. Not one.

Vic found an empty chair and sat down.

Behind the brightly spotlighted lectern, Hank orated like a tent pole evangelist, his black sunglasses raking the audience. "Each Sunday in youth group, I recounted my weekend of drunkenness and debauchery, sin and madness. And I begged, *begged* God for mercy."

His t-shirt advertised "LikeReal.net." Was this all a recruitment racket? Vic squinted around at the walls but saw no LikeReal posters anywhere.

"My friends listened with the unholy fascination of kids being told a ghost story at a campfire. I will lay my hands on the holy bible and swear to you these religious youths were thrilled, my friends, *thrilled* by the vile details." Hank wiped his sweaty forehead with the back of his arm.

"I can still picture their faces. But if any of my old peers were standing right here in front of me, I could not see them so clearly now. For, one terrible night, a night like this with hot devil winds, my eyes were taken from me—one three-quarters blind, the other gone entirely." Someone in the audience gasped. "But it was not my place to ask 'Why? Why did I drive? Why did I drink? Why was it raining? In the name of the Holy Spirit, why did this terrible thing happen to me? Has God forsaken me?'"

A "preach it, brother" came from the back of the room.

"I tell you; it simply does not matter. Because every bad thing teaches us a lesson, and every loss teaches us to cherish what we have not lost. I thank you."

LIKE REAL

As Hank stepped out from the lectern, he clipped its edge which sent his walking stick clattering to the floor. Nonetheless, he graciously bowed to the smattering of applause.

House lights flicked on, cueing the audience to herd over to the snack table.

Meanwhile, Hank shuffled around, arms reaching out for the lectern, and from there, leg and foot rooting around for the stick, which was only two inches out of his range. Vic jogged over to him, picked up the stick and gently grasped Hank's arm.

"Let's get ourselves to the snacks."

"Thank you, kind person." He sniffed the air. "Eternity by Calvin Klein?"

"You're good."

"God opened a window."

As they neared the table, their pathway opened wide. Most of the audience had already selected their pastries and now stood in line for coffee and punch. A few nodded at Hank, as though he could see their validation.

One dude said, "Good job, brother, lots to think about." He held a glazed twist, Vic's favorite.

"Thank you for the kind words, friend," Hank replied, as Vic steered him to table-side.

First things first, Vic got himself a glazed twist, then leaned to ask Hank: "Old Fashioned? Glazed? Chocolate frosting?"

"Surprise me, then let's you and I go talk outside for a moment."

Vic nodded okay and picked a chocolate.

Outside, moth parties on the halogen lights created interesting shadows on Hank's face. Vic had never talked to a three-quarters blind person before, and kept his eyes glued to the reflections of the lights on Hank's glasses.

"Will you take a look at my new eye, and describe it to me?"

Vic hadn't expected this, but if it was the preamble to a sales pitch, then bravo. "I'd be honored. Go for it."

"I wouldn't ask such a thing of a complete stranger, but I want the objective opinion of someone who doesn't know me well enough to lie."

"It's no problem," Vic said before taking a last bite of donut.

"Whatever you see, however horrible it might be, be honest."

"Okay."

"I swear to sweet baby Jesus, I can take it."

"Let's go." Vic didn't try to hide his impatience.

Hank removed the glasses. His right eye looked real, albeit cloudy and unfocused; the left one was a gleaming silver robot eye. *Good goddamned thing he wears those shades.* This was the type of sci-fi peccadillo that created panic at the farmer's market. "How much per pound for the eggplant?" "Holy shit! A robot. Where is your owner?"—"No-no-no, I'm a real guy with a scary robot eye who just wants to make ratatouille!"

"Well?"

"It could use a paint job."

"Fair enough."

"How long have you . . . "

"Almost two weeks. But in a few days, I'll be able to see shapes."

Vic nodded a congrats.

"May I ask about your difficulty?"

"I lost most of my hand."

"Combat?"

"In a sense."

Hank waited for elaboration. But Vic sipped his coffee, sensing a pitch coming his way.

"Well, you should get in touch with Doctor Cord, his name is Doctor Kenneth Cord, and he is a miracle worker. I'm living proof. Go to LikeReal.net. The URL is on my shirt."

"So, are you the official spokesperson?" Vic asked, baffled as to why *this* guy, with his disconcerting eyes, would be marketed so robustly, and not, say, Sgt. Joan, who would not only be a better example of successful handiwork, but also bring a little military-borne speechifying to the table. Was it the religious angle?

Hank looked thoughtful, as thoughtful as a guy in shades could look. "I'm not official, no. But I've been giving inspirational talks for years, and now I have a new angle, and once the eyes grow and function, I will have yet another angle." He sat back in his chair, gazing up at a light that maybe his one-quarter eye could see.

A big wind wrested a frond off a palm tree, skittering it along the gravel. Vic acknowledged this as a sign that all interesting nights must end, and said goodbye, after Hank assured him he had a Lyft on the way, and it was okay to leave him at the curb.

Vic got into his car, with a last glance at Hank standing by the curb, backlit by the sign, head tilted as though watching for the Lyft. *Next week he'll see their headlights bright and clear.*

He remembered the first time he watched *The Terminator*. The image that unglued his shit more than anything was when Terminator drove the gas tanker until it exploded and blasted fireballs, incinerating the truck. Sarah had barely escaped, but just when she calms down, because for sure he's dead, Terminator rises from the flames, a full metal skeleton with red devil eyes.

In light of current possibilities, Vic speculated whether a new hand from Doctor Cord would grow more realistic in a matter of months, or if it would look like the Terminator's skeleton hand? Or Hank's eye? How would *that* play at the farmer's market? "This eggplant feels a bit overripe"—"Hey, stop squeezing the produce with your scary robot hand, weirdo!"

Vic pushed the start button with the lone thumb and reached over with his left hand to shift from Park to Drive.

7.
DOCTOR CORD

THE FREEWAY WAS way too congested, so Vic hopped off in Lincoln Heights, driving through the industrial corridor outside Chinatown, a chunk south of the 110-freeway sprawling out into a plain of train tracks, shipyards and warehouses. A two-minute eagle's flight to Dodger Stadium, and one of the few areas in LA where you might spot a tumbleweed or the rumored pitbull pack and the lady you hope still feeds them.

His attention to the landscape filtered out thoughts such as percentage breakdowns of his motivations: curiosity vs desperation vs business opportunity. *You gonna get a robot hand, aren't ya?* But the GPS voice cut in, advising he should "turn left in 500 feet."

Vic took a last look at the Elysian Hills, recalling an article he read about how, from 1959 to 1962, an army of construction workers pulverized the Stone Quarry Hills, pushing eight million yards of earth and rock to clear the way for Dodger Stadium.

He made a left into a wide alley, lined on the right with warehouses, and on the left by a ten-foot wall acting as a barrier between the alley and train tracks.

"You have arrived at your destination."

The warehouse, distinctive from the dingy grays and beaten whites of other warehouses because of the pearly paint job and slight geodesic curves, would fit perfectly in the middle of a vast desert . . . an alien compound camouflaged in the landscape. Still it was a giant rectangle, the largeness of which was both intimidating and a cause for hope. They must have money because they are successful and do good work.

He parked in front and got out, amazed by the entrance doorway, a two-paneled model. Laser-etched in the center was the foot-hand-eyeball logo. On the roof, a small round camera. Topnotch tech from where he stood. A self-conscious reflex of late, he made sure his right sleeve hung down below the lone thumb.

Vic was about to either turn back to his car or knock, when he heard a whirring noise coming from around the side of the building. He stepped to his right to investigate. Emerging from a small open door at the side of the warehouse was a three-foot tall silver robot holding a cube of compressed garbage in its clamps as it glided across the alley to the dumpster. Its body rose, revealing two silver legs which elevated it high enough to drop the cube into the dumpster.

Vic checked his watch: 10:02 am.

The robot lowered down to its previous height, then rolled back into the warehouse. The door sealed shut behind it. *Huh.*

A voice behind him said, "Basic automaton on wheels."

Vic whirled around to find a man in his 60s wearing a leathery tan under his lab coat and movie star smile. Doctor Cord.

"So elemental that I can repair him with a little duct tape and spit." Doctor Cord laughed: "ho-ho-noo-hee-hee." Weird, right off the fucking bat. "Doctor Kenneth Cord, please call me Doc or Kenny," he said in a mellifluous baritone. His baby blue turtleneck tucked into high-waisted slacks gave him a 1970s catalog model vibe. At the end of the day, he probably replaced the lab coat with a double-breasted blazer and a yachtsman's cap.

Cord stepped towards the front doors, and they

whooshed open a la *Star Trek*. Awesome. Weird. Mostly awesome.

Vic followed him inside, into a reception lounge right out of the original *Logan's Run*, with a blazing white couch, a boomerang coffee table and an aqua rug with zebra stripes. Seated behind an elegant glass desk was a handsome man in his twenties with a big grinning mouth and the dead eyes of a machine.

With a sweep of his arm, Doctor Cord presented him to Vic. "Allow me to introduce you to Stephan, my office manager." Vic's knees got a little gummy at the presence of a real-life robot in human form. He'd seen plenty of sex robots in pictures and Canadian porn, but never in real life, and never an office manager.

Stephan stood up. He wore a nice suit with a minty green turtleneck. Extending a milky hand for a vigorous shake, he said, "Hello, Victor Bonjovi Moss; how are you today?"

"I see you got a few of my stats." Vic faked a laugh, unsure whether to address the statement to the robot or the doc, finally choosing the robot. "Even the ones I don't readily advertise, Stephan."

Stephan corrected him. "Stephan." (Steff-ON)

"Stephan." (Steffen)

"Stephan," (Steff-ON) the robot said in the same balanced tone.

"Right, then." Vic shook off the creeps, vowing to persist, to see how this'd shake out, and wondering about the other two-paneled door behind Stephan marked "Private."

Doctor Cord cleared his throat. "Follow, please," and marched across the white low-pile carpet to the private door which, of course, glided open, splitting "Private" into "Pri-vate."

They went from carpet to black shiny linoleum; a perfect surface for the Doc's Croc sandals to make syncopated walking noises. Vic suspected this was all a prelude for a song and dance number with body parts as back-up dancers, but Cord simply led him down a long dark hallway, a quasi-mine tunnel—with an occasional cubicle here and there—lined with LED sconces highlighting invention displays mounted on tables.

Doc stopped abruptly, turned to his right with a squawk of the Crocs and approached a display shelf occupied by a big brass robot head. "My first," he said, running his finger down its metal nose. "Eighth grade metal shop. At the time, I was possessed by a love of Victoriana and so created something that Jules Verne might have written about."

Vic whistled appreciatively. "How much does it weigh?"

"25 pounds. Like a fat chihuahua . . . ho-ho-noo-hee-hee."

Vic should have fled. If this guy thought Hank would be a good brand representation, he was out of his flipping mind. Was using Hank a niche marketing tactic targeting the religious? Or the true gullibles so narcissistically addled they couldn't help but come for a visit? *Gullibles like me.*

Doctor Cord droned on about the head's capabilities. Vic chided himself for spacing out and snapped to attention.

" . . . and it would turn its head to the left, and then to the right, and to the left, and to the right . . . then back to the center."

"It's magnificent." Vic followed another ten feet before Cord stopped again.

"Mop shoes," Cord announced. Yep, a pair of mop shoes on a small pedestal with its own light, and a framed patent behind it. "You put them on, you place the cleaning strip onto the Velcro, and you 'Mop While You Walk.' My invention. Screwed on the patent."

"My grandpa got me those for Christmas."

"I saw none of that money." His Crocs shrieked as he pivoted back to the established route.

Halfway to that other door. To Vic, itching to get to either the Doc's point, or to his own pitch, it was unclear whether that door was the ultimate goal, or why he wanted it to be. Maybe because it was so far away, and so curious and shiny.

Cord stopped again in front of a silver, oversized human hand. "Here we have the prototype for Proto, a prosthesis that will revolutionize prostheses forever after."

Vic found himself face-to-face with its titanium tendons and clear plastic "veins." *Terminator*. Should he just go with a flight response? Bid adieu to the mad scientist, zip down the hall as fast as he could, say, "Have a super day" to the robot in the lobby and shoot out the fucking air lock? Or . . .

Doctor Cord lifted the prototype off its stand and tried to hand it to Vic, who backed away. "It is adaptive, sir." Cord was clearly miffed. "Proto analyzes the recipient's DNA to grow matching skin and then links to the brain by tapping into the neurological algorithms."

So here's the pitch. Vic allowed Cord to place the metal hand in his left hand. *He knows I need a hand. Either my long sleeve disguise is bullshit, or Stephan did some deep-dive research.*

"That's terrific, the adaptation and all, but I guess you misunderstood my call earlier. I'm a programmer and a designer, and I'm here because I can improve your site, with, like, real non-flash animation, which by the way has been dead for a while, because I promise you nobody's going to sit through a 10-second page load."

Doctor Cord wiggled out of his Crocs, pulled up his trousers and waggled his bare feet at Vic. One, then the other. "Tell me, Victor, which is real?"

One was a typical tanned man's foot, the other a typical tanned man's foot with a few more extruding veins. Gray veins. Well, wires. Vic pointed at that foot.

"Fair enough," Cord said a bit sheepishly. "I've only had it for six weeks. I estimate full assimilation in a week or two."

Assimilation! Why that word? Vic's arm hair spiked. Any Borg references did that to him. He handed Proto back. "What if things don't work out, does it . . . can it be removed?"

Doctor Cord's eyes flitted towards that door at the end of the hall, an easy field goal away. "There is a kill switch—more precisely, a kill button—that renders the prosthesis inert."

A kill button? Vic didn't enjoy the sound of those words together. He offered a business card to Doctor Cord. "I can fix your site. You'll get better retention rates with speedier load times. Amazing tour. Loved the trash robot outside."

Vic was backing up, almost to the mop shoes, when Doctor Cord pulled a handkerchief from his lab coat pocket with the flourish of a magician and let it flutter to the floor.

"Watch, Victor." He extended his fake foot, squinched his toes around the hankie, tossed it up and caught it. Vic almost applauded, guessing it was pretty awesome that a fake foot could clench a hankie. "Imagine what a hand could do, young man." Cord's eyes locked on Vic's saggy sleeve and single thumb.

It took all of 15 seconds for Vic to bid adieu to the mad scientist, bolt down the hall, wish a "good day" to Stephan and burst out of the front doors. As he dashed to his car, he vowed to start jogging, and to learn how to accept things he could not change. Was that how it went? Whatever, true love, if he ever found it, wouldn't fizzle because of a few missing fingers. Why did he ever believe that?

The Honda roared to life, and he zoomed down the alley in the same direction as that truck. *The key to life,* he thought, *is utilitarianism and not aesthetics. It's simple code that gets the job done and doesn't grandstand with unnecessary flourishes.*

He hung a left, knowing his metaphor didn't work since fingers were more than fancy umlauts of the hand. *You gonna get a robot hand, aren't ya? No.*

The sight of the hills through the windshield calmed

him. That night, lights would radiate behind those hills from the valley floor, where the Dodgers would hopefully beat the Royals in a night game.

8.

THE GEORGE MODEL

Exercise goals:

1. Incorporate wind sprints into nightly walk (good for Number One, too)
   —Nailed it, shot for three out of seven, did four.
   —Next step: aim for four 10-yard sprints. PER WALK, weak bitch.
2. Pushups. Work up to five in a week.
   —Failed it. Did one. Thumb collapsed. Had to rest.
   —Next step: Do two. Thumb must build strength.

Grooming goals:

3. Wipe your ass better. Do not take this for granted.
   —Didn't Nail or Fail. Lefty improves daily. Relies too much on baby wipes.
   —Next step: Keep at it. Left hand must build muscle memory.

Administrative goals:

4. See a real doctor about a new hand.
   —110% is keeping the third and final appointment.

***

The building came into view when Vic turned left on Olive and started up the slight grade. It was hard to miss: eight stories towering over a neighborhood of homes, condos and churches. Built in the early 1960s, it sported groovy blackout windows and white honeycomb framing. To an architect in those days, this must have looked quite futuristic.

He found a parking space three long blocks up the hill, which added 568 more steps to his 10,000-per-day goal. Killing It would be 9,000. 110 percent would be 10,000. People might have a hard time with the math; but his formula factored in expectations and the passivity infecting a guy once he's failed. So, getting a 70 percent goal rate wasn't as cool as setting the goal for 60 percent, then achieving 70 percent, thus killing it.

One percentage he was certain of: he was 100 percent sure the new plastic hand extension wouldn't compensate for Thumb's ineptitude.

Norman paced at the edge of the building's small parking lot, having nabbed a space in their six-dollar lot. Vic noted the receipt tucked in his shirt pocket, and also Norman's big, supportive smile. Today he wore the Willie Nelson braids under a Dodger cap. He patted Vic on the shoulder. Vic shot him a wan smile. They both admired the reflection of the towering palm trees in the upper windows before going in.

The elevator was original. No upgrades here. Max occupancy was 2,100 pounds. Occupants today: three old women, and Norman and Vic. It felt crowded.

"Are you going to wear it out of the store today?" Norman said.

The old biddies' conversation ceased; Vic now had a rapt audience. "Maybe. If they got all the measurements right."

The elevator dinged on four, and the ladies shuffled out.

Norman waited for the door to shut, then said, "All you need to do is learn to type with a few of them and the thumb, and we'll be back in business. Segwaying to Coffee Bean solo is no way to Segway, bub."

"Aww, you miss me."

"Of course I do, little buddy."

Ding. Next stop: six. They alighted onto a carpeted landing with zero windows and four doors, and entered the door labeled *Doctor Zaharian, MD*.

As he did when visiting the dentist, Vic wore earbuds and listened to classical music during the procedure. From his perch on the exam table, his eyes scoped posters of prostheses adorning the walls while Doctor Zaharian fitted a gray plastic hand base around the stump and cinched it tight.

"This will function as the dorsal and palm," Doctor Zaharian said. Only Norman heard her. Vic was still in the land of Bach and prostheses. Attached were four plastic fingers. A small belt originating from the base of the new index finger wrapped around the thumb with an adjustable Velcro attachment.

Vic smell her perfume. Hell, he could taste it. *What's she hiding?*

"We are done," she said loud enough that Vic heard.

He removed the earbuds. His face couldn't hide the creeping disappointment as he surveyed the gray plastic fingers tapering to rubber pads on the tips. It reminded him of the C-3PO gloves he wore on several Halloweens. On the left side of the index finger were two tiny white buttons.

"Use the thumb to activate the phalanges to curl or straighten," Zaharian explained.

Vic pushed the top button, but nothing happened.

"That makes them rise up. However, they default to up, so you must first push down."

Vic pushed the bottom button, and they folded down.

"Keep the thumb on the button until the fingers reach their desired position," she said.

Vic curled them back into place. He glanced at Norman in the guest chair, eyeing the prosthesis over the top of his reading glasses, over the top of a gossip rag. A real Norman Rockwell moment. "Not bad," he opined.

"Not great," said Vic.

"It'll steer a Segway."

Vic sighed.

"If you wish to have more realism, you want to get the Alexander model, the doctor said. "But that is out-of-pocket, plus the remainder of your deductible."

"How much?"

"If you had VA insurance. If this were a result of war, which, it was not . . . yes?" She opened his file, scanning the particulars.

"No . . . I was there, though."

"It is all expensive. It is highway robbery. But I am not in charge."

"You're not Doctor Zaharian?"

"I am, my dear, but the insurance people are in charge."

Norman dog-eared a page before closing the magazine. "What are we talking, numbers-wise?"

"Yeah, can I see the picture again?" Vic asked.

She nodded and fetched the sales binder from the sink area next to a jar of cotton balls, then opened to a page and held it up for him. Norman squeezed in for a look.

The Alexander model featured realistic skin and drawn-on nails and knuckle wrinkles. *50 percent more realistic,* thought Vic. But it had those same two buttons on the index finger. And the price tag was 8,500 dollars.

"I'll think about it." He held up his new contraption. "What's this called?"

"What you have now is the George."

***

As they waited for the elevator, Vic and Norman heard the sounds of people laughing behind one of the four doors. "Birthday," Norman guessed.

The lights above them quivered for a millisecond as the elevator lumbered down from the floor above. When it opened, Norman dropped a motivational bomb: "'We can always choose to perceive things differently. We can focus on what's wrong in our life, or we can focus on what's right.'—Marianne Williamson."

"Thanks, Skipper," Vic said as they stepped inside, then immediately pressed themselves to the opposite wall of a woman and a toddler. The woman wore office casual scrubs and a key badge with the name *Sasha* on it. They passed the fifth floor. Sasha could easily play a horny dental hygienist from Alberta visiting the big city for the first time. Vic's eyes floated south to the toddler; a little girl clinging to her mom's legs. Pigtails, face brimming with terror as she gaped at his new hand extension.

Before Vic wrestled control of his idiot mouth, he'd engaged with her, playfully raising the George model. "Aargh, I'm a pirate! I lost me hand to a hungry shark!"

The toddler burst into tears. Sasha scooped her up. Vic made a move as if to apologize, but Sasha kept her eyes glued to the descending floor numbers. They passed two. Then a hard landing. Norman and Vic hung back to let the pair leave first, then skulked through the lobby and out to the lot.

"Go ahead, mock," Vic said.

Norman put his hand on Vic's shoulder. "Sometimes the fun idea is really the bad idea, know what I mean?"

"I do. But for every ten fun ideas that become bad ideas, two of them turn out to be good ideas."

Norman looked ponderous, twirling a thin braid around his finger. "Beautiful point," he conceded before throwing back his head, tearing off the Dodger cap. "Aargh, I'm a pirate and a seagull ate most of the hair atop me head."

Vic scowled up at the palm tree reflections until Norman finished cackling. "Thanks for coming. See you at work—with this." He thrust out the plastic George model.

Norman shook it. "Focus on what's right, little buddy."

9.
THE LUMBERJACK

THE LIGHT TURNED from yellow to red. Cars around him ran the red. Ah, the Los Angeles commute. Vic stopped, knowing he was the better person than those runners. He definitely had better hair—which he confirmed in the rearview mirror. Exceptional, without a doubt. The rest of him was regular work-day Vic: dark rinse jeans, a crisp t-shirt that smelled like fabric softener, and a 90s sitcom bad-boy blazer.

He'd released the hem on the right sleeve, hiding most of the prosthetic, except the tips, which joined Lefty's fingers on the wheel.

Green light. Merging traffic. Cars crept along Hollywood Way. Vic watched an Air Alaska jet rise then disappear into terra-cotta clouds.

Less than a month ago, an IPO was on the horizon. Would it be any closer now? Bossman Chet, a pompous prick, had a moment of grand generosity the day an angel investor kicked in 1.2 mil and everyone drank champagne at lunch. During the celebration, Vic happened to be in the john pissing next to Chet when Chet leaned over, glancing at his dick—not in a come-on, but in a "mounting you as the mightier animal" way—and said, "You're in for 10,000 shares."

Vic's stream did a double take. "Really? That's, uh, thank you, Chet." They shook their boys in tandem.

LIKE REAL

Chet beat him to the sink. "Listen, brohah, it's only an 8-dollar strike price. We're gonna jam it up to 80 bucks by Q2 of next year. Mark my words."

Vic took his turn at the sink. "No doubt. We're all committed to making this thing kill, Chet," he said, realizing Chet would fall in love with *Killing It 110% and Beyond*. Type-A predators were the target audience, not the more Captain America scenario he'd imagined, where a virgin wimp became a hero. What had he created?

"The trading window opens after a year." Chet placed his hands under the deafening hand dryer.

"So, I guess we should try not to fuck it up for a year." Vic enjoyed his brave joke, even knowing he was a puss for cracking it in the safety of the dryer noise.

Silence. Chet sniffed his fingers, then said, "What was that?"

"I said, 'we're going to ace it in—'"

"Heardya the first time, sucka," he said, opening the door with his pinky and slipping out with a smug grin.

Traffic cleared, and Vic got up to 35 MPH. He guessed the IPO was still a speck on the horizon, as he'd neither seen nor heard about the promised shares. This, more than any other reason, including a paycheck even, prompted his return to work earlier than planned. The goal was to get a written promise, or the shares themselves, within a week.

The first person he saw inside was Keisha, the bun-head receptionist. She waved at him but continued her phone conversation. " . . . being a tactile person is no excuse for putting her hands on your man's . . . "

Vic escaped, preferring his own version of her next word. He entered an open floor plan, sticking to the perimeter as he headed to The Hive, his face frozen in a neutral half-smile, eyes averted from everyone, and prosthesis in his jacket pocket.

He arrived at a door labeled as "The Hive." A service window to the right of the door was open, revealing the Help Desk-er on duty: Sunil, who rarely spoke to anyone beyond the necessities of their computer issue; if he wasn't working on someone's laptop, he wore headphones and watched soccer on his own. Vic nodded. Sunil nodded back.

Once inside, it took a moment for Vic's eyes to adjust to the utter darkness punctuated by computer lights. When he regained his 20/40 vision, Norman was already in a hug stance.

"Welcome back!" He wrapped his string bean arms around Vic's shoulders. "We have donuts." He pointed to a pink box on Vic's desk.

Sunil joined them, hands stuffed in his jean pockets. A short, unknown young woman wearing a parka and braids with choppy bangs grabbed a glazed twist.

"Is this my replacement?" Vic asked.

"I have a name," she said, gobbling the top off the twist.

"This is Amy, our intern," Norman answered. "She was going to be here, with or without you. Where do you go to school again, Amy?"

Amy spoke with her mouth full. "Cal State Northridge, Computer Science with a minor in Game Design." Vic glanced over to her screen, noting the paused anime RPG.

"An impressive endeavor," Norman said, snatching the apple fritter before Vic could get to it. "That one's for me. You can have anything else."

Amy and Sunil each grabbed another, leaving Vic a chocolate with sprinkles and a plain Old-Fashioned. No milk. Great fucking start.

"Hey, we're Swiss Army buddies," Amy said, shaking her wrist where hung a bracelet with a dangling sheathed knife. She pointed with her donut to his, resting by his dog tag.

"Wow, that was a super special moment," he said.

"Is that sarcasm, dude?" For a 100-pound squirt, this kid was ready to rumble. "I love sarcasm, it's the sheee-it. And so are you."

"Oh, now—" whatever brilliant quote Norman had on

deck was interrupted by the door opening behind them, spilling bright light into their darkness.

The silhouette of Keisha said, "Attention, mole people, Chet wants a quicksee with"—a long nail sabered through the air, landing on Vic—"you."

She closed the door. Once Vic blinked away the intrusive fluorescent burn on his retinas, he trudged out, certain he was marching to his doom. Norman patted his back on the way, saying, "While Chet speaks, you might keep yourself cheerful by thinking of all the karaoke-ing we'll be doing tonight."

On his trip through the maze of mostly empty cubicles, the chatter of a few dozen worker bees abated. Vic grew self-conscious at the covert voyeurism directed at him, and the squeaking his shoes made as he walked.

Chet Masters, CEO was etched on the door. Male voices on the other side. Sounded like they were watching a football game. Vic reached for the door handle with his right hand. Damn. *Don't accidentally shake his hand,* he thought, switching to Lefty and entering Chet's domain.

Mercedes catalog on the credenza by the door—check! Midlife-crisis Chief Operating Officer, aka Frat Fuck, sinking a Nerf ball into the hoop by Chet's enormous desk—check! Chet in his Herman Miller chair—check!

"Toss it here, brohah!" Chet raised his pink piggy arms.

Frat Fuck winged it at Chet; the ball sailed over the head of Darla, the elegant HR lady, seated in a guest chair scrolling on her phone.

The chair next to her contained a manila envelope labeled V.B.M. *That's what I am to these jerks, data in an envelope.*

Chet sunk the shot. Of course. "Nice one! Remote high-five coming your way," said Frat Fuck. "I'm outtie for the call. You going to jump on?"

"In a few." Chet's rat eyes shifted to Vic, who picked up his envelope and sank into the chair. Darla rested her phone, and both she and Vic sat at attention thinking the meeting had begun. Chet held up a stumpy finger, "one sec," and jabbed a text. *No doubt sending a dick pic to Frat Fuck.*

Vic glanced at Chet's Word-a-Day calendar, displayed outwards for his guests to see. Today's word was "anthropomorphism." Vic leaned in closer for the definition.

"It means if you think animals or other inanimate objects are people," Darla explained. "You know those sad women who buy realistic baby dolls and treat them like actual infants? I saw this tragic documentary about three—"

Chet banged the phone down on his mahogany desk. Meeting time. "Listen up," he said, as he began rhythmically squeezing a racquetball. "Two lumberjacks are in the forest chopping down trees. One jack takes short breaks throughout the day. The other jack takes no breaks at all. None. Nada. Nunca. Tell me if you've heard this—"

"I've heard it," said Darla. Vic wanted to laugh. That was balls.

"Not you." Chet's ruddy face burned hot.

Vic, understanding Chet needed to tell the story in full, said, "No," and forced himself to look interested.

Chet smiled. Probably the same face he used when he squashed a bug. Or someone's dream. "By the end of the day, the jack who takes periodic breaks has cut down way more trees than the other jack, who takes no breaks. And, of course, he's all kinds of pissed. He goes, 'How did you do more work than me in less time? What do you do on break?' And the other jack says, 'I sharpen my ax.'"

Darla made eye contact with Vic, shooting his mind back to an office Halloween party when she came as Pippi Longstocking with a toy plushy monkey pinned to her shoulder, striped stockings, and a red wig with braids akimbo. As people got loaded, they tried feeding the monkey peanuts or scotch, or demanded it to dance, basically fucking with the monkey until Darla fled to an empty cubicle to cry and remove it. Vic, who dressed as the

Hamburgler, had solicitously unpinned the monkey for her, which resulted in a moment where they might have kissed, had a Nerf rocket not banged into the side of his head.

"You can't fire me for a disability," Vic said.

"No one's getting fired." Chet abandoned his ball to sift through a stack of mail.

"You promised me options, will that still happen?"

"Nothing's changed. We only want you to take some more time."

"Sign where I put stickies," Darla explained, nodding to the V.B.M. folder. "It's two weeks on full pay; if you're out longer, you'll use vacation time, and when that runs out, you'll get 60 percent of your salary via worker's comp until you return. Chet, you also have a copy to sign."

Chet glanced at the form. "Victor Bonjovi? How did I miss this?" He sang, as bullies did throughout Vic's life, "I'm your cowboy, on a big horse I ride. All the ladies want me, whether dead or alive."

Dipshit couldn't even get the lyrics right.

"I'll see you in a few, then." Vic stood, stepping over the Nerf ball.

"There'll be plenty of trees for you to chop down when you get back," Chet said, adjourning the meeting by swiveling around to shred a piece of mail.

On his way to the door, Vic mumbled under the grinding: "Or put an ax where my hand should be."

10.
TOYS & COSTUMES

AFTER CHET TOLD him to go home, after he met his replacement, Amy, and before his life changed again, two bells on a ribbon tinkled together when the door of the toys and costumes shop opened, and Vic glided into a quaint wonderland lit by strings of tiny white lights. There were no customers, only a kindly old woodworker perched on a stool, whistling as he whittled.

No, no, no. The Percocet was lying to him. He was in Costume Superworld. Former aircraft hangar. Bright as a bank of stadium lights. Retro game music. Packed with shoppers. 62 degrees. Vic shivered and squinted, turning a half-circle from the cart area to customer service. Where in the hell would he find the perfect gloves? Not too puffy, not too tight, not too bright.

Luckily, a gentleman Orc waved at him from the greeter podium. "Hi, can I point you in the proper direction?" He ended on a big smile that didn't seem fake. Vic wondered if the striations of blue on his skin were permanent or semi-permanent. Whichever the case, his near palpable benevolence calmed Vic down so he could focus.

"Gloves? I'm looking for." *You sound like Yoda. Fix this.* "I need gloves."

"Race Car Driver? Or more Darth Vader-y?" He came around from the greeter podium, looming seven feet tall in his four-inch platform boots. His name tag identified him as Gorbag.

"Uh, black. Not too puffy, not too tight, not too bright?"

"We also carry Thor gloves," Gorbag said. "But they only come in gray. Well, silver." He held his hand to his mouth, whispered, "Gray," and rolled his eyes.

"Do you have something sort of between race gloves and gardening gloves?"

"Old timey-garbageman! Leather, sturdy. I swear we used to have some." Gorbag's neck didn't simply swivel to the various aisles of merch, his entire body turned as one. "You know what? Try aisle four. You'll also find cowboy gloves and gauntlets there."

"Thank you." Vic took off in the exact wrong direction. A double whistle got his attention. Gorbag pointed the other way, Vic waved at him with Lefty. "Thanks again!"

As he strolled the no-shit 200 yards to aisle four, Vic speculated on the karaoke evening to come, 80 percent sure Norman knew Chet was 99 percent going to fuck him out of options. And, if that were true, he'd be duty-bound to inform his "little buddy." Also, hiring an alleged intern to do his job added up to a minor betrayal in Vic's opinion, and Norman would answer for it tonight.

He'd also be forbidden from singing "I'm Never Gonna Dance Again," because he always wound up in freak city, crying and emoting, and people—women—the saddest women—extolled his brilliance, bought him drinks, or gave him their number, which would then give birth to "Drunk Norman," a creature who abandoned his Zen chill to a tidal wave of ego and vomit and tears. He loved every version of Norman, but Drunk Norman was a pain in the ass.

***

Inside her half of a pretty duplex, Tanya listened to ambient jazz as she futzed with her computer. "Fucking wine bar music," Connor would scoff after shitting on one of her story ideas, then rephrase it as his own. Story pitch days always tested her grace under fire, because even if there wasn't a hint of competition for story space, Connor would find a way to create it.

Nobody, not even that asshole, could deny the heady lure of a Human vs Something article. What better than spiders? The evergreens remained, like the lady with a roach in her ear, or the tiny fish that swam up a man's urethra. But new classics were always the goal. The Lone Thumbman with his multiple bites and amputation had all the hallmarks of a potential classic, including the squirmy feeling that runs up the spine, and the pity.

Six tiled windows on her computer featured photos of spider carnage. Humans with soupy cheek holes, skin rot, gnawed-on eardrums, exposed bone. What she wouldn't give for pictures of his wounds. Now was the time to re-establish contact with the subject, Victor Bonjovi—ha—Moss. She'd have to change his name. Hugo Whitesnake Stone?

***

Back in Costume Superworld, Vic browsed gloves. Lots of gloves. Black fringe gloves, which could be cowboy or stripper-cowboy, or biker or stripper-biker. Race car gloves. Ooh. Ski gloves! Not too padded, but the green neon details were attention-drawing. *Why don't people have ski parties anymore?* he thought. *Crackling fire, brandy, wind-burnt cheeks?* Percocet world was so comforting.

His cell buzzed. Lefty pulled it from his blazer pocket and balanced it in the palm of the George model. Here was a text from Tanya!

Hi, you owe me 45 dollars plus a big tit.

He smiled.

Another bing. Another text: *TIP*

He poked out a slow reply with Lefty and got as far as *not only will I, when* the fucker slid off the George model and landed screen-side down on the linoleum.

Vic bent to retrieve it, grimacing at the cracked screen. "I sent it, didn't I?" Yep. Sent "Damn." As he stood up, defeated, he spotted the "Police Duty" gloves. Not too big, not too small, jet black. We have a winner, folks! He plucked it off the display hook. Size XL. Perfect.

"There he is," came a woman's voice from somewhere down the long aisle.

Vic acted fast, thumb pushing the down button on the George, one eye on the fingers' achingly slow descent, the other on a security guard striding towards him. Beef-muscle, military-short haircut. Why was George so slow? "Crap." Vic had forgotten to charge the prosthesis last night. The fingers weren't even half folded yet, so he shoved it deep into his blazer pocket.

At five yards out, the buzz cut security guard lifted his chin at Vic in a nonverbal declaration that he had Vic in his sights. Fucking Pyle, that's who he brought to mind! Huge, psychotic Private Pyle from *Full Metal Jacket*. An enormous homicidal monster. Jesus Christ. Vic backed up a few steps, trying to keep cool.

Behind Pyle was the voice, a redhead in a *Sailor Moon* costume. And bringing up the rear, an agitated Gorbag. All eyes rested on Vic's pocket, its thin linen doing zilch to hide the outline of something big and not carbon-based contained within.

"Hello, sir, how are we doing today?" Pyle asked rhetorically. An aggressive pat on Vic's shoulder. The other hand rested on a holstered taser.

"I was doing okay, I found these . . . "

"Drop it, sir."

Vic dropped the gloves.

"Whatcha got there in your pocket?"

Vic pulled the George model out into the open, careful not to excite Pyle.

Sailor Moon stepped in for a closer perusal.

"That's far enough, Greta," Pyle warned.

"Well, it's not a weapon." She popped her gum. "And I guess it's not our product."

"What did I tell you guys?" Gorbag wailed.

Pyle's eyes twitched. "Are you certain, Greta?"

"Yeah. Sorry."

"This is my prosthesis," Vic explained. "I lost four fingers and most of my palm. I keep it in my pocket, so it doesn't upset anyone." He pushed the down button again. Every eye stayed on the fingers until they folded. It was a long five seconds.

Gorbag gave him the police duty gloves for free.

***

Tanya got tired of staring at her phone. No further reply came beyond *Not only will I. Will you what? Apologize? Explain? On the record? With images*? She reached for her notebook of ideas, flipped to an empty page, and scrawled in pencil: *when humans rot.*

***

A *Family Feud* rerun from the teens played on Vic's 60-inch screen. Number One, perched atop the coffee table trunk, yipped every time a bell or a buzzer went off. Or when Steve Harvey mugged at the camera. The George model lay abandoned next to Number One.

Vic was in the bathroom, securing the police duty glove to the stump by wrapping it with black duct tape. He squirted some cologne, checked the hair in the mirror, rested the glove on his chin like Will Riker making eyes at a holographic lady. "You sing like an angel, but I bet you fuck like a demon."

"Name something you don't want your mate to bring to bed with you," Harvey asked.

"Problems!" Vic yelled towards the living room.

A woman's voice said, "Another person, Steve." Laughing, clapping. More laughter. Number One yipped. Harvey must be making crazy eyes at the camera.

Vic adjusted the longer jacket sleeve over the glove. "Let me see 'another person,'" said Harvey. BUZZ. The audience went, "noo." And Vic's phone tinkled with another Tanya text.

Was there a second half to that sentence?

Vic considered his response. She had every right to an answer. *If I could find a place where I could wear gloves . . . maybe one of those Victorian cosplay deals Norman goes to . . .* He knew it shouldn't matter. If someone likes you, they don't let a recent amputation sour their—

A male contestant said, "Problems, Steve!"

"Let me see 'Problems.'"

BING! Number One yip-yipped. Lefty slid the cell into his pocket.

***

Vic sailed down the stairs into the building's courtyard. Pool lights made silhouettes of the Barbies as they tossed a volleyball across the shallow end. Cozy, wearing her life jacket, missed a crazy-high toss and the ball soared over the pool gate. Vic kicked it back in a spray of chlorine.

"Thank you!" Both sisters waved.

***

Why Norman thought dressing like Bing Crosby was a good idea was anybody's fucking guess. Plaid golf cap, paired with tweed pants and a polo shirt? Apparently, Norman's target demo tonight was "Lonely Academic Spinster."

"Who's this fella?" Norman gestured to the glove as he got in the passenger seat and belted up.

"Is it too obvious? Is it the first thing you see?"

"First thing I saw was the seat upon which I now sit," said Norman. "And then I saw the glove, but that was a straight line. I imagine a lady might first notice your beautiful eyes."

Vic raised the glove. "Phantom middle finger." Norman plugged in his phone and put on his Karaoke Playlist.

Vic gunned it as "SexyBack" started. Norman did a fine Timberlake impression.

***

Inside the red-lit karaoke bar, shadows sitting around tables paged-through song books. Up on the tiny stage, Norman sang "SexyBack," and it was creepy as fuck.

Nonetheless, he had a small dancing audience, including Vic and a woman in a leopard print dress, who semi-twerked when Norman slid into a grating falsetto for the bridge. " . . . Dirty babe . . . "

***

Later at the bar, Leopard Print Dress half-listened to Vic pontificate, but mostly fixated on his glove, which had come loose. Her nails crept across the bar towards it.

" . . . links all of your exercise, diet, calendar and goal apps, and each is weighted with a score," Vic said, trying not to hear Norman singing "I'm a Lineman for the County." "And then it tallies up your weekly progress and gives you the . . . "

Leopard Print Dress finally yanked off his glove with a giggle—the shock at seeing the plastic hand almost knocked her off the stool but for the wide backside of a dude wearing a sideways baseball cap.

"I'll take that back," Vic said, avoiding eye contact.

"Oh my God, I'm sorry, I thought you were some kind of cosplayer I didn't understand, I'm so sorry," she said, handing Vic the glove, then, to Baseball Cap. "And thank you."

Leopard Print smiled at Baseball Cap as he backed away, a love-struck Romeo, hands to his pecs, then out to her, tossing his heart. Vic had used that move on more than one occasion. She smiled, slurping the remains of her margarita.

Her sucking sounds redirected Vic's attention to a memory of Tanya's lips—sucking on a straw, then speaking to him: "I want another Chi Chi. Do you want another Chi Chi?"

When he returned from the memory, Leopard Print had vanished. He slid off his stool, leaving the glove on the bar, and waved for Norman with his very long thumb.

No music played on the ride home. Semi-Drunk Norman told him, "Life isn't fair, and nobody's perfect. To understand that is to be content."

LIKE REAL

"Life was plenty fair to some people," Vic said. "Tom Brady, Tom Cruise, Tom Brokaw, Tom Ford, Tom Landry, Tom Holland, Tom Petty, Tom Jones, Tom Hiddleston, Tom Selleck . . . Tom Hanks, Tom Hardy. Life is more than fair to the Toms."

"Tom Mix, old cowboy star," Norman said.

"Did you know I was getting benched today?"

"You weren't benched, you were given time off."

"You hired somebody."

"She was already coming, Vic."

"Life isn't fair and nobody's perfect, I guess."

"Tom Thumb had a shit life."

After dropping Norman off, Vic drove straight to Doctor Cord's warehouse.

11.
MEET PROTO

OH MAN *a second-door visit,* Vic thought, following Cord out of the lobby, into the long hallway, and down to the mysterious door. No stops along the way.

The doors parted, admitting them into a laboratory. Not a cubicle. A "Laboratory" in a Vincent Price voice, complete with banks of computers and bubbling liquids in beakers. Still, this didn't faze Vic.

In a nook behind them stood a dentist's chair with an enormous light above it, and an instruments table with one of those new paper-thin computer screens he'd read about. Brand new tech. Not bad.

At the far end of the room loomed a huge metal desk. The nexus. To its left, the robot doggy door. Vic wondered if Cord patted Trash Robot on the head as it went on its garbage run.

Cord led him to the desk, to a release form. Vic felt heavier, slower as he sat down, his eyes breezing past a bank of red buttons at the right side of the desk. A pen appeared. He lost peripheral vision, seeing only the letters he struggled to write with Lefty. *Am I high?* He flashed to that moment a few minutes back when he passed Stephan's desk and Stephan sprayed something in the air. He thought it was air freshener and how amusing that a robot endeavored to sweeten air it could not smell.

Vic stopped signing at *Victor B Mo*. "Did Stephan dose me?" he asked.

"A gentle mix of Valerian root mist and a tinch of chloroform," Cord replied.

"Then why am I even bothering to sign consent?"

"While there is no substitution for proper forms and releases, on the phone you gave your verbal consent to the operation and everything that entails," Cord explained. "Those were my exact words: 'all that entails.' Even pre-surgery requires some anesthesia. We gave you a small amount, as they do at hospitals, meant to calm the patient prior to—"

"Yeah, I'd probably wig out on the Hammer Horror vibe otherwise." After enjoying a brief fantasy image of Tanya sucking on his real-looking fingers, Vic finished signing.

In the blink of an eye he found himself strapped in the dentist chair, which hummed as it unfolded into a surgery table. Doctor Cord cupped his nose and mouth with a breathing mask.

Hallucinations began immediately. The lone thumb transformed into a pulsating chrysalis torn asunder when a butterfly emerged in a splatter of cocoon juice. "Do you want another Chi Chi?" the butterfly asked him. It wore kitty-cat glasses and the face of Tanya. Vic reached for her with his right hand—a metal claw-like thing fused to his wrist and thumb.

"What the—?" He rocketed to consciousness, found himself sitting upright in the chair in partial darkness. The big overhead had been turned towards the wall. Vic raised his right arm into its beam.

Behold Proto, hand-completer. Wires connected the flesh of the thumb stem to the four cyborg fingers and wrist. Terminator emerging from the fire. A cyborg's skeleton. Vic yelped, tried to leap out of the chair, but the leather belt across his hips stopped him. "Hello? Doctor Cord? Doctor?" He unfastened himself, holding Proto out to the side with no idea what to do with it. The doors whooshed open, and Doctor Cord entered, a living Creamsicle in his orange turtleneck and white pants.

Stephan followed behind him, in a near-identical outfit, but also holding a glass of green glop, which he offered to Vic's left hand.

"Hydrate," Cord said. "It's a smoothie."

Vic accepted the glass; sniffed it. "What's in this?"

Stephan smoothly listed the ingredients as, "Kale, banana, apple, spinach, flaxseeds, chia seeds, almond milk, ice."

"And what else? Are you dosing me again? No thanks." Did Vic try to set the glass on the instrument table? Or did he mean to drop it on the floor, where it shattered and splattered?

"Sorry." Vic swung his legs off the chair, stomped his feet awake. He and Cord regarded each other from either side of the green mess. "Am I free to go?" Vic asked. "You're not gonna charge me after promising me it's free."

"Young man, listen to me. All of this difficulty you went through? So did I. However, I received my Proto with only localized pain mitigation because I needed to stay conscious in order to give directions to Stephan."

Vic squinted over at Stephan, who nodded an affirmation. "Well, good for you, tough guy." Vic backed away from the glop, stepped around to the other side of the surgery chair.

"This powerlessness over a physiological mishap, well it's atavistic," Cord said. "With science, we control much of our physiology, and someday, perhaps all of it, and death would then come only by way of catastrophe."

Vic, still trying to figure out how to get around both android and master, gave a start when Trash Robot glided inside the lab with a trash bag. Everyone shifted to accommodate its wending trip through the laboratory to empty waste baskets into his stomach-compactor, compress it to a cube, then exit via the doggy door.

"I'll need you to email me a copy of everything I signed," Vic said, drifting towards the door.

"Flying below the radar, whether intentionally or unintentionally, is the only way real scientific leaps and bounds become possible," Cord said. "You and I and others are part of something miraculous. Yes, it can be worrisome. But I'm here to tell you it's possible. I was glad to be Patient Zero. And while there is no shame in traversing this world with an artificial appendage, if you had a choice, would you want it to be obvious to everyone? The first thing they see? The thing about you they'll never forget? Wouldn't you rather exist without noticeable handy-capable body parts?"

"I'll need an instruction manual," Vic said.

"Stephan will give you a pamphlet," Cord said. "But honestly, the best method is to issue simple commands. Verbal, at first. Come back in three or four days and we can begin official training, yes?"

"Miraculous or whatnot, I have a feeling, uh . . . you said there's a kill switch?"

"Victor, it's a baby. It will evolve. Look at my foot."

"I've seen your foot already way too many times."

"Look closely. There's hardly a difference."

The wires had settled, barely rippling the skin, and could pass for real veins. Still, time to go.

Stephan matched his pace down the hallway. "You'll need an instruction pamphlet, Victor."

"Shouldn't you have worried whether someone was driving me here?"

"That is not in my job description."

"Shouldn't the doctor have worried? When someone comes out of an operation? When someone has anesthesia, shouldn't the doctors make sure he doesn't operate a vehicle?"

"I will get the pamphlet." As Stephan turned to his desk, Vic hustled out the front door, squinting in the bright morning sun, fishing keys from his pocket. Stephan's voice echoed from the speakers in the empty alley: "You forgot the pamphlet, Victor. Please return for your pamphlet," The doors opened. Stephan waved a pamphlet. Vic grabbed it and stalked to his car. "Shall we set your next appointment?"

"I'll make one soon." Vic unlocked the car.

"Wednesday, 10 am?"

Vic spoke to Proto. "Fingers curl to palm." Nothing happened. "Phalanges fold to palm." Boom. The fingers moved fluidly into position. Vic raised the hand in a thumbs-up. Real thumb seemed so pink and boring next to the shiny new exoskeleton.

"Have an enjoyable day, Victor."

12.
GETTING TO KNOW YOU

VIC THRUST HIS face under the shower spray. Lefty slicked back his hair, and Proto joined on the other side, its metal phalanges slithering over the scalp. Pinky Proto nicked his hairline and blood dribbled down his forehead.

"Belay! You need some padding." Vic scraped scalp skin and hair follicles off the pinky. "How 'bout you fetch the soap?" He pointed to the shower caddy. Proto tentatively reached for the bar of soap, but it slipped away. "Watch and learn."

Proto rose to a proper vantage point, undulating like a cobra. Lefty deftly retrieved the soap from its caddy. "See how it wants to squirt out? You need to spread the phalanges to block all escape paths." He released the soap back into the caddy. "Now it's your turn, but make sure—" Proto impaled the soap on its index finger. The other fingers closed around it, their precise edges furrowing into its soft back. Vic chuckled doltishly as it soaped his chest.

***

Japanese tribal drums played loud enough to shake his windows. Vic, shirtless and in his flowy black kendo pants, stood before his bladed katana and two wooden bokutos. "Pick one," he told Proto, who went straight for the katana. "No. This is practice, we use the bokuto." Proto lifted a wood sword from its mount. Mentally, Vic commanded:

Give it to the other hand. Proto obeyed. Holy shit. Here was a milestone. Goal exceeded by at least 130 percent.

"I practice in order to mold the mind and body, to cultivate a vigorous spirit." Vic bowed. "Ki-ken-tai-ichi!" He and Proto moved through a series of thrust, strike and sidestep poses, working their way around the room. Number One scampered into the kitchen as they neared.

Vic realized he'd given no mental commands in the last minute or so, yet he and Proto worked as one. Goal exceeded 170 percent. Unfortunately, no matter how hard he focused on the moment, his phone on the couch, open to Tanya's text, vexed him.

Why is she single? She's smart. Employed. Runner's calves, Vic thought.

Could be her choice, he answered.

But she chose to go on a date with a semi-stranger, which suggests some level of desperation.

Yeah, what's that all about?

She must be mental.

Yeah, mental.

Say it like a British guy.

She's men-toll.

The sharp pain in his Achilles tendon prematurely ended their practice. Vic lowered the sword and hobbled over to the couch. "Music off." The beats stopped. Vic massaged the tendon with Lefty. In this moment of all-encompassing pain mixed with depression mixed with Percocet, Proto wouldn't stop flexing open and closed, keeping rhythm with Vic's thumping heart. Louder, louder, until it filled his head—until he heard the dance music coming from downstairs.

***

The YouTube video that appeared via the search phrase "kendo sword fighting" began with a camera panning across at least 50 young students in a dojo, wearing black robes and kneeling, butts on their heels, foreheads on the floor. A voice-over said: "Kendo, derived from the ancient

Kenjutsu, aims to mold the human character through the application of the principles of the katana."

The video froze on the students as they uniformly rose from their kneeling positions and sat back on their heels. The image zoomed in closer to a particular student in third row center: Vic! Young, perhaps 14.

"Hello, kendo boy," Tanya said. She texted: *Hello????* *Frowne*d. Deleted the last three question marks before sending.

***

Down by the pool, Cozy and Mamie danced with other Barbies and a few Kens. Everyone held coconut drinks. Two Korean businessmen stood on the outskirts smoking. A brunette in a bikini pushed a Ken into the pool, but he grabbed her hand, and she tumbled in after him. "Oh God, I hope you lose your bra," Vic whispered from his vantage point behind his blinds.

He basked in the warm and fuzzies, until a cold metal intruder touched his jewels. Vic bucked and hollered. That fucker Proto had dive-bombed down the front of his flowy pants, cupping the whole shebang. "Release them! Release! Belay!" He yanked Proto out with a grunt. "You could have scraped me! Rule time, motherfucker." He opened the LikeReal pamphlet to read the Five Suggestions . . .
* *Set rules immediately*
* *Use positive reinforcement*
* *Make explicit Verbal or Mental commands*
* *Eat healthfully*
* *Avoid alcohol and drugs*

"Since we're copacetic with the Kendo, rules shouldn't be a problem for you," Vic told Proto. "So here's rule number one: do nothing until I give you a verbal or mental command. And if it's mental it must be specific, no 'Mmm, I want that cookie' and then you snatch it for me. The command is 'Grab the cookie' or 'Put the cookie in my mouth.' Basically, do not act on the desire until I've issued the command."

71

Proto twitched. "Rule two: as with all sentient machines, do no harm to humans. Three: obey the safe word, which is 'belay.' When I say 'belay' you stop whatever you are doing until the next command."

Proto remained still.

"And the last but most important rule is you go nowhere south of my belly button unless I have given a verbal, not mental, not inviting imagery, a *verbal* command."

Proto and thumb formed an okay sign. Vic nodded, placated. Then a buzzing sound whipped him around. A text from Tanya!

"We hooked her, yes we did," he sing-songed as he read her text: *Hello?*

Yes, he should have responded by now. How long had it been? Since before Proto . . . three days? *Here's something you can help with*, Vic said to Proto mentally. *You hold. Thumb types.* Proto scuttled around to clutch the cell from behind.

Vic texted: *not only will I pay u back, I'll buy 100% of next dinner.* His left thumb touched the Send button but did not depress. Proto twitched, as if impatient. *Let's see where we are in a few days, then we'll revisit. Another few days is a dick move, but within acceptable limits.*

A voice in his head that wasn't his but sounded identical said, "Weak."

***

Vic let Proto start the car and work the gears. Man and machine were so in sync that while idling on the 110, Vic daydreamed about being in a steamy atmosphere, in a garden of vines, sitting across a bistro table from a beautiful woman who was not Tanya. A woman who was clearly attracted to him. "Let's just get this on the table right up front," fantasy Vic told the woman before plonking Proto down on the table so hard the wine glasses trembled. "This is my cyborg hand, Proto. We're a package deal." The woman's eyes widened, but not with disdain. "And the little dog, too." Fantasy Number One, on a chair beside him, yip-yipped.

***

Half-buzzed from the pain meds, Vic announced himself at the door, and then sidled into Cord's reception room and waved at Stephan behind the desk. No response. Stephan's eyes were open, but jet black. He swept his hand past Stephan's face to confirm he was powered off. Would it have killed them to give him a screensaver that simulated shut eyelids?

The interior doors parted. Doctor Cord already had his Crocs off and his pant leg up. "Look at this!"

"Wow," Vic said. The foot looked real. Utterly real, if hairless. "Let me see the other one."

Cord pulled up the other pants leg, also hairless. "Identical, yes?"

"Sure."

"Today is your big day." Cord nodded for Vic to follow as he stepped through the double doors.

"Is Stephan rebooting or something?"

"Oh, yes. Stephan: activate!" With a rustle of polyester blend pants, Stephan joined them. The destination: a cubicle already bedecked with a light, a camera, and a blue screen backdrop.

"Stephan will record everything, along with the cameras, for double proof of your progress," Cord said. "Please stand before the screen. Do not smile. Neither should you look somber. A simple neutral expression will suffice."

"I don't, uh, I don't remember a 'before' shot," Vic said, skin prickling at the creepiness of Stephan's unblinking attention.

"We took one before the operation," Cord assured him as he stepped behind the tripod. "Move your eyes to the space between my camera and Stephan's head." Vic obeyed. "Now, hold up Proto, phalanges spread, as if saying 'hello, friends.'" Again, Vic did as he was told.

Stephan leaned in, eyes on the hand. "Flesh patches, the bulk of which has appeared on the index phalange. Also, nascent nails."

"What's your skin made of?"

"Silicone and additives, Victor."

"What's my skin going to be made of Doc?"

Cord's mouth curled into an assuring smile. "Carbon and other proprietary elements."

Later, Cord and Vic sat at a small conference table in a different cubicle. Stephan, seated across from them, had his amber eyes trained on Vic as Cord demonstrated knuckle-rolling a quarter. Cord's pale and sweaty face was hard to ignore.

"Are you okay?" Vic asked.

"Perhaps I'm getting a cold." Cords eyes wandered the room as though reacquainting himself as to where he was. Stephan re-focused his camera-eyes on the doctor.

"Doc?" Vic cleared his throat. "Doc?"

"I lost my foot while ice camping," Cord said, eyes glazed with a hard memory. "Frost bite. My boot broke. There was a storm. I sat in my tent for three days. One by one, my toes turned black. My phone didn't work. My food ran low. I made small fires. I waited." He cleared his throat, then looked down. "I did an unspeakable thing." Was he choking on tears? "It nearly broke me. What a person does to survive . . . I'm sure the ice would have taken my whole foot and then started up my leg . . . had I no pickaxe."

Oh God. Whaaaat? "Then I guess it was a good thing you had one," Vic said.

Cord snapped out of his reverie, placed a quarter atop Proto's index finger. "Tell him what you want him to do. With the proper vocabulary."

"Phalange one up, move it to phalange two and up, then to three . . . oops." Vic repositioned it. "Back to one . . . roll it. Good! Keep going! I'm doing it! I'm doing it!"

Doctor Cord clapped and laughed, "ho-ho-noo-hee-hee!"

LIKE REAL

Stephan joined him, "ho-ho-noo-hee-hee!"

Vic laughed, too. *Fuckit, this ain't insane, because I'm Future Man and Proto can knuckle-roll a quarter! Ho-ho-noo-hee-hee!*

13.

CRUSH THE CAN

ARMED WITH A can of—"Spider Blaster"—RAID in hand, Vic tore duct tape off the bedroom door and burst in, ready to dispatch any scuttling thing with extreme prejudice. Anything that crawled, flew or nested was probably already gone, thanks to an already deployed can of bug fog on the floor smack middle of the room. Vic opened the window a crack to dissipate the eau de insecticide, then selected a jacket-t-shirt-skinny jeans ensemble. He was running at 85 percent thanks to pain meds and dark roast coffee. He'd achieve one-hundred percent if he simply remained at work until the end of the day. No more forced time off. And the only thing he'd be signing was ownership of his big stock grant.

He left Proto unsheathed. The new skin patches gave it a mottled texture, but he was not about to let a glove inhibit this growth spurt. He practiced in the full-length mirror how to best hide Proto in his jacket pocket, then kissed Number One goodbye and headed to work, brimming with confidence.

Vic spent the commute fantasizing about Proto grabbing Chet under the fat pink chin, raising him a foot off the ground, slowly crushing his windpipe until he sobbed and pissed himself. Then, lowering him back to the ground to give him a tiny stab of hope that maybe it's over, and maybe he'll get to live after all. FUCK NO. Vic jabbed sharp phalanges into Chet's piggy neck, slicing through tendons and veins until the metal fingers encircled the spinal cord, throttling it until he heard the CRACK—then sawing through the flesh in a spray of blood until head and body disengaged, and Chet's body collapsed to the floor. Vic-torious Proto raised the head like Salome with John the Baptist and slam-dunked it into the Nerf hoop.

Vic parked into a space marked JMS Consulting and strode into the reception area reeking of confidence. He smiled at Keisha.

"Hey welcome back!" she said.

"What's up, doll?"

"I got adult braces." She bared her teeth at him, showing off an old-school metal mouth.

"Lookin' good. I got a new hand." Proto made the devil sign, and Vic strutted out, cock of the walk-style.

"My lord," Keisha said, spinning back to her phone.

Inside The Hive, four desk chairs met in the middle of the room, and all lights were on for inspection. Vic extended Proto like a woman with a new engagement ring for Norman, Amy and Sunil to marvel at. Everyone ignored the beeping noises coming from Norman's computer.

"It's going to be a coding champ with a short ramping-up period," Vic boasted.

Amy somehow had a magnifying glass in hand. *Fucking Nancy Drew.* "Flesh is growing . . . wow."

"We are witnesses to adaptation, guys." Summing it up prophetically was why Norman was a successful middle manager. Amy handed him the magnifying glass; he went in close, eyes widening at the smattering of fleshy islands and the veins, which even from a foot's distance, you could see were transporting blood. Norman shook his head so hard his scraggly ponytail whipped his shoulders. "Skynet," he whispered.

"Please don't go there, Norman," Vic said.

"I always go straight to Dystopia, don't I?"

"90 percent of the time you do. I mean, pointing out the worst possible scenario isn't tough love. It's mean."

"Are you a 6-year-old?" Norman asked, clipping Amy's burst of laughter by handing her the magnifying glass and a warning look.

"Sometimes, yeah," Vic admitted.

"Well, here's the take-away," Norman said in a summation tone. "Machine and human collaboration is why we have jobs."

"That's your best?" Vic said. "How about 'this is a glorious step for humankind' or something?"

Norman nodded thoughtfully. "All right, everyone, let's take a half-minute of silence to celebrate adaptation in all its bewildering permutations."

Vic closed his eyes. He'd take that. Adaptation. It's how anything survives. He could hear everyone breathing, and the beeps from Norman's computer, but otherwise the group kept their heads bowed and their mouths shut for 30 seconds.

Sunil cleared his throat. "I wonder. Which is the stronger hand?"

***

Norman and Sunil segwayed along the designated walking paths. Vic traveled groundside with Amy, the cocky little job thief.

"Did they tell you?" Amy asked him.

"Tell me what?"

"They hired me. I'm a Programmer. Full time. Nobody told you?"

Vic shrugged, trembling on the inside as they arrived at the "Green Space," a micro park rimmed by hedges. "Will you continue pursuing your degree?"

"Ha-ha, just kidding, freak," Amy said before skipping over to sit on the stone bench next to Sunil.

A teenager had diagnosed Vic's insecurity and exploited it for a joke. Little did she know the damage Proto could do if wrapped around her windpipe. Or if it pitchforked her. *Vic the Impaler*.

Norman handed Amy and Sunil cans of soda, which

they snapped open and guzzled. Amy finished hers first and raised her hands in victory. They both belched.

Vic took position in the middle of the space. Sunil and Amy raised their phones. "No and no," Vic told them.

"I agree," said Norman. "Phones down. Record it in here." He pointed to his head. "Experience life as it happens, kids."

Amy and Sunil nodded, handed their cans to Vic, who raised his arms to the side at shoulder-height.

Norman counted him down. "Four, three, two, one, go!"

Lefty squeezed tight, but not much happened. Proto remained inert. Out loud, Vic said: "Do it!" In his head: *Come on! Crush the can. Close around it. Yes, it's counter-intuitive, but obey me. Please? Please crush the can.*

"Let's go fellas!" said Norman.

"Crush those motherfuckers!" Amy cried.

At last, Proto activated, annihilating the Mountain Dew can in a half second. Lefty shredded and bled as aluminum tore into flesh.

Everyone cheered. Vic stuck Lefty into his armpit to stop the bleeding, feeling pretty fine otherwise.

Then, like diarrhea at a birthday party, Chet showed up, steering his Segway down the walking path. He passed by, then reversed, coasting back to glare suspiciously at the group. On cue, everyone nodded or waved, and got up to return to work.

Except Vic, who moved not an inch.

Chet raised his jumbo Frappuccino in a "cheers" and resumed his journey.

Proto dropped the can, wiped itself on Vic's pants, pulled out the phone, and accessed the prepared text to Tanya: *not only will I pay u back, I'll buy 100% of next dinner*

Proto's gooey index pad hovered over Send, awaiting Vic's orders.

"Make it so, Proto."

14.

AN INVITATION

THE STONES' "The Spider and the Fly" was playing as Vic's text landed on Tanya's phone. His response time had been three days. *Not bad*, she thought, *considering what he's dealing with*.

She had imagined no response other than: "hey, let's talk about my horrible experience on the record and I'll let you use some super disgusting pictures taken in the ER." But dinner? What hijinks might ensue? Would he, in a bid to impress her, tear the tablecloth off the table? Or perhaps when the bill came, she'd hear a penny whistle as he pulled his pants pockets inside out.

***

Vic parked in front of Doctor Cord's warehouse, checked his phone for the 20th time, then tossed it on the passenger seat next to Number One, whose attention was on the trash robot as it glided across the alley then back through its little doggy door. Vic's watch said 10:03 am. Everything ran on a clock at The Lab.

Outside the car the wind picked up, deporting bits of trash from grittier alleyways into Cord's pristine space. Vic got out, zipped his windbreaker using Lefty. Squinting against the dry Santa Ana gusts, he was almost to the door when Stephan's voice crackled over the loudspeaker. "Hello, Victor, the doctor is not seeing any patients today."

"Oh. Is everything okay?" Vic yelled up to the camera.

A pause, just long enough to prickle the skin. "Yes, Victor."

"Can I . . . what about Zoom? Can I Zoom him?"

"When the doctor is feeling better, he will be in touch, Victor."

"Any idea how long that'll be?"

"Not with any certainty, Victor."

"Got a guess? Two days? Three days? A week?"

"I am unable to guess, Victor."

Vic stepped on a 7-Eleven sandwich wrapper before it wafted to the door. Was he being watched? Would they think he was the litterbug?

"Goodbye, Victor Bonjovi Moss."

"Goodbye, Stephan.

"Stephan." (Steff-ON))

"Stephan." (Steff-en). *Fuck that guy. Machine. Whatever.*

This was a bummer, especially in light of recent developments. In three days, Proto had sprouted a thick skein of "skin" with denser clumps in places, and the beginnings of nails. Plus, there was the awesome kendo symbiosis. With such positive things happening, it was a shame he still had to hide it from others.

From her.

He got into the car. His cell buzzed with a text.

From her! *Not spam. Click Here.*

Vic's click delivered him to a coupon for a free Kundalini class. Saturday at 10 am. Four days to grow skin. Was this a goal he should even log since it was out of his control? He clicked into the *Killing It* app and typed into a "goals" box: *yoga gloves*.

BING. Tanya again. This time the text read: *please come.*

"Oh, I'll come, all right—right, Number One?" But honey boy was asleep on his back.

***

"You know how you're always asking us 'how many ways can we pull apart this piece of fruit?'" Tanya asked her editor Cindy over the phone. "Obviously, the first thing we do is re-categorize the story and include it in other listicles—"

"I prefer calling it 'the examination from every angle, a gyno with a flashlight and a speculum,'" said Cindy, a 35-year-old who spoke to people as if she were a bawdy old aunty.

Tanya screwed up by prefacing instead of leading with the meat. The result being several hundred seconds spent listening to Cindy croon about how alpha reporter Connor's interview with a former child star netted six listicle ideas and the possibility of co-authoring the child star's unauthorized autobiography. Whoopie, a byline on someone else's autobiography. Also, "unauthorized autobiography?" Did the child star have a second personality? Ugh, the constant adulation of that arrogant baby mustache mofo Connor was exhausting.

"Listen, Cindy, I found a local guy who lost his hand to spider bites," Tanya said.

A smoker's gasp. Cindy didn't smoke. Fucking poseur.

"I have quotes from a hospital insider, too. And here's the big hook: I was on a date with him when it all started. I. Was. On. *A date*. With. Him."

"Dear lord in heaven up above, you got yourself a first-person confessional," Cindy said. "A pot-boiler, baby. It's sizzling fists to the gut. Pa-Pow." Tanya knew better than to interrupt the monologue, instead picturing the square Elaine Stritch glasses, the blunt bob and slash of crimson on Cindy's lips. "The Holy Grail. The perfect goddamned storm." Cindy stopped to make gulping sounds. Probably Chablis. "Do this. Do it well. Do it like a courtesan."

"How is—how do I—?"

"Tease us skillfully. A lot. Then, *deliver*."

"That's the plan."

"I need something by Wednesday."

"Can I do a series?"

"Let's see what you give me by Wednesday."

15.
HANK'S EYE

SEATED ON A bench outside the community center, Hank swatted flies away from the fresh bandaging over one eye.

"Everything I love dies. I got drunk the night after my dad's funeral and my eye died. Then my mom died. Years go by, and I'm blessed with a new eye, and a kitten, a little skinny speck of happiness. Purred every time I touched him. He got out. I found his head on the sidewalk. Must have been a coyote. He was four months old. I left the door ajar for a split second. Then I spent all night . . . it doesn't matter, it was my fault. He'd been fostered since he was a newborn. He knew only love. He loved to attack my slipper. Nothing was its enemy. Until he met his enemy, and it ate him."

Hank curled over, weeping. Vic, swollen with empathy as he pictured a coyote's killing bite on Number One's neck, rubbed the top of Hank's head, running Lefty's fingers through wiry auburn locks, feeling idiotic, but instead of stopping, he leaned into it by making soft cooing noises and saying, "It's okay, it's okay."

Hank finally straightened up, dabbed the near-blind eye with his coat jacket, waved off a fly. "I went to bed with 20-70 vision in the prosthesis. I was starting to see the shapes on the moon, too. My vision was sharp enough to record every bit of the horror on the sidewalk."

Vic murmured more condolences about the cat, which Hank didn't seem to hear.

"There was a sharp pain, perhaps a terrible headache, so I called Doctor Cord, but his unholy gatekeeper told me he was ill and that I should take aspirin. I woke up to intense throbbing. I opened my eyes and I saw shadows. Only shadows. I thought it was the grief. Or a stroke. I raised my hands to wipe away the sleep boogers. Instead, I found blood clots and severed veins."

"They couldn't put the eye back in?"

"I'm sure they would have been able to do so, had they found the godforsaken thing. The police and the hospital people searched my entire apartment." He dug into his pants pocket, bringing out a meticulously folded handkerchief to dab his runny eye. Vic noted he was not wearing the LikeReal.net t-shirt. "It mystified everyone. Did someone break into my apartment and cut it out while I slept? Or did it simply up and roll away?"

***

From the crack under Hank's closet door, It peeked outside, where shoes padded by on the low-pile carpet— white shoes, black shoes, brown shoes, a pair of which pivoted, facing the closet, then approaching.

It retreated as the door opened.

A click, then the halogen light bathed everything in a yellow hue. The brown shoes nudged other shoes aside and sent a cane toppling. A female voice called out to someone; seconds later, a pair of black tactical boots entered. Another click and a flashlight beam raked the floor, pausing on spaces between laundry, boxes, suitcases, shoes.

As the beam swung closer, It rolled backwards, with passing views of a woman in a windbreaker, a uniform cop, the halogen light, the vinyl floorboard, and the thousand-watt beam, which missed It by a hair.

***

"I suppose I'll learn to live with one eye. And no cats," Hank said.

"Aw, you can get another one . . . when you're ready."

Hank nodded, bucking up. "Well, praise God for the limited sight I still have, and for His help in keeping me from dwelling on loss."

"Amen to that."

Hank clapped both hands around a fly, smashing it.

"Hey, you saw the fly."

"I did it by sound." He flung the body into a bush. "Come back as a butterfly, dear creature." He wiped his hands on his handkerchief. "May I see your progress?"

Vic pulled up his sleeve. Hank moved in for a squint. It was his turn to blanch at the wires and spotty skin growth. "It'll get better," he told Vic in an unconvincing voice.

Vic nodded, throat softening as though readying for a big boo-hoo-hoo, but he swallowed and composed himself. He still had two days till Kundalini. And yoga gloves to buy.

16.
PAINT JOB

"HOLD STILL,**"** Amy said. "I don't want to get this shit on everything." She held a coffee cup filled with beige liquid, stirring it with a small paint brush as she hovered over Vic, who sat front-and-center in The Hive. "Ready?"

Vic didn't answer. His spookily lit face came courtesy of a desk lamp placed on a stepping stool to better light Proto, stuffed into a fingerless yoga glove with fingers poking out in manicure position.

And although Proto was chunking up with skin, the fingers still looked like Deadpool's face brindled with wires.

His audience from afar was Sunil, and up close, Norman, always the supervisor, nodding his agreement with Amy.

"Close your eyes and think of an empty beach," Norman offered.

Vic went to the deck of the Hoo Maru, feeling the ocean spray as the great ship cut through the sea, but Proto's jittering continued, forcing Vic to mentally scream *chill the fuck out!*

"Yay or nay, I've got a backlog of work," Amy said.

Vic glared at her a moment before turning to Norman. "Remind me how my replacement is suddenly a make-up artist?"

"I took a class on how to make masks," she said.

"At the Learning Annex?"

"Was that an insult? Cuz I don't know shit about the Learning Annex, but I'll go look it up."

"And then what?"

"Shush. Shush," Norman said. "Future-world problems require the ingenuity of youth, so let's respect the effort and settle down."

Vic stink-eyed the gooey liquid in the cup. "What is it, exactly?"

Amy sighed. "A little o' this, a little o' th—" Proto shot out, closing around the cup, and Amy's hand. A humping power move that rendered everyone silent. Even Amy's screensaver music seemed to cut out.

"What, exactly, is in it?"

"Crayons, liquid latex, and a little of my grandma's pancake makeup," Amy said through clenched teeth.

"You may continue, Amy." Proto released her.

"Did we just witness a singularity?" asked Norman, who then made significant eye contact with everyone on his team, including Vic. "Did we?"

"No, I gave the command," Vic replied. Norman sat back, not entirely comforted.

Amy wiped paint clots off the brush on the edge of the cup, and everyone held their breath as the brush touched the index finger.

Proto kept still, calming Vic, which allowed a relaxation wherein he could imagine the many Kundalini positions Tanya might help him get into.

"Done." Amy fanned the newly painted fingers with her hands. Norman followed suit. Vic avoided looking until Amy and Norman stopped.

Oh God. The fingers could double for rotting pork ribs.

"I'll paint on some fingernails if you want," Amy said. Vic didn't respond.

"You did great, Amy," Norman said.

Sunil put his headphones back on and disappeared into the service room.

Vic didn't stir, even when someone removed the desk lamp. Soon, muffled techno Ren Faire music announced that Amy had resumed her RPG.

17.
KUNDALINI

CLOSE YOUR EYES. Focus on your third eye. Inhale deeply . . . exhale . . . inhale. Ong namo, guru dev namo."

A dozen voices responded: "Ong namo, guru dev namo."

Vic, on a mat in a corner, mouthed the words as he peeped through his lashes at Tanya, up at the front in yoga capris and a tank top showing off her yummy hibiscus tattoo.

A breeze through the open window puffed the gauzy curtain so it lapped the edge of his mat. Vic scooted forward a little, adjusting his position to match everyone's: cross-legged with a hand on each knee. He figured he was far enough away to risk resting Proto on a knee. The yoga glove helped obfuscate the horror, but if someone looked closely enough, the fingers would raise questions.

"Breathe deep. Hold your breath and set your intentions for the day."

He saw her notice him and slammed his eyes shut.

"Now exhale. Ong namo, guru dev namo."

The students, including Vic, repeated, "Ong namo, guru dev namo."

"What do you want to achieve? See it, feel it, and know it is yours." To this, Vic opened his eyes, and she hers, and they locked. Proto rose a few inches from the knee to behold her beauty while pulsing like a beating heart.

***

Later, as students rolled up their mats and Tanya namaste'd them goodbye, Vic loitered, hiding Proto by tucking him under the rolled-up mat he held under his arm. Lefty clutched a flyer.

The place emptied, except for an elderly man up front, asleep on his mat. Tanya shut the door and got on her cell, scrolling as she turned to Vic. "How did you enjoy it?"

"I loved it . . . blissful."

Her eyes remained on her phone. "You'll become addicted; I promise."

"Maybe I already am." He didn't let that one linger and instead proffered the flyer.

She stopped her scrolling to accept it, smirking a bit at the 1990s band flyer quality. "A Birthday Celebration" was written in pink letters above an image of the Barbies in matching sarongs.

"They're sisters who manage and maybe—nobody knows for sure but maybe—own my building.

"Twins?"

"No, it's one of their birthdays. I don't remember which. Anyway, there's food, drink, music, a pool. You can meet my dog."

Tanya handed Vic her phone. "Is this you?"

Vic skimmed the crime blotter item about his trip to the ER, nodded, cleared his throat, wished for the miracle of a perfectly executed explanation to satisfy her and make her want him. Instead: "I know the party is late notice, so I'll understand if you can't make it—oh shoot, your money. I got it, don't worry."

Lefty dug into his pocket and pulled out a wad of folded bills, which he handed to Tanya. "I didn't bring a wallet. But it's all there. With a big tit." Joke-fail silence ensued. "Cuz . . . a little throwback there."

"Would you consider telling your story?" Tanya asked. "I just need a couple of quotes for a medium-sized blurb. I mean, I hope for more, but I'll accept just about anything."

Vic nodded, backing himself toward the door. "I'll think about it over the weekend. Hope you can come tonight. Cool class. Blissful, as mentioned," he babbled, while thinking: *Stop being a pussy. At least stop talking. For the love of God—*"Stop." Oops. That was out loud. Tanya froze. Vic, paralyzed at the door, could do nothing as Proto shifted the mat to Lefty and smoothed back Vic's exceptional hair. Tanya was far enough away that the fingers were indistinct, if oddly colored. "I didn't mean you. Um, I'm not usually this . . . way," Vic sputtered. More silence followed until broken by a whale of a fart.

Vic and Tanya jumped, eyed each other suspiciously. Finally, snoring sounds brought their attention to the elder Kundalinian snoozing on his mat. Relief washed over them both, and they shared a smile.

"That's Mr. Lake," she said, as Vic slipped out the door.

Tanya watched him go, then strolled over to the sleeper, waving the air to dispel the fart essence. "Time to wake up, Mr. Lake." She used an app on her phone to produce a little yoga gong and his eyes opened.

***

In the car, Vic barked at Proto like a drill sergeant. "Who told you to think for yourself? Who told you to show yourself? Who the fuck said you could move? I run this fucking show called Vic Moss. Slick Vic. Vic the fucking boss."

Man and cyborg man-hand, inches from the other, were both poised to strike. Vic was not above biting and gnashing. Proto seemed ready to Alien-facehug him. Neither moved, neither stood down, until Tanya emerged from the building, and the face-off ended so man and cyborg man-hand could ogle her, then drive home.

18.
PARTY PREP

BUILT IN 1968, Vic's building resembled those new-vintage complexes choking every square inch of Hollywood with one bedrooms renting for four grand. Vic felt lucky to pay 2900 bucks, a trade-off for living in the nethers. A shock of purple and magenta bougainvillea crept up the entrance wall, tickling the bottom of the aluminum cursive letters spelling "La Villa Armada." An aluminum schooner above the building's name, tarnished by northeast wind blasts, still gleamed when the rosy beams of sunset hit it.

As the sun fell below the building's roof and its courtyard dipped into twilight, Cozy and Jun-ho were hanging a "Happy Birthday" banner on the rails by the pool gate. Jun-ho had exchanged his business suit for casual pants and a shirt without a tie. The lime green shirt he wore was testimony to Cozy's predilection for couple's dressing, since she was decked out in a lime green sarong.

Mamie's fella, Yeong-jin, still in business pants but also wearing a wife beater that clung tight to his wee potbelly, lugged an extension cord and two battery-powered tiki lights downstairs. Mamie followed in a utilitarian one-piece suit. Her contribution to the decorating party was the pool light she held.

"Here's the birthday girl," Cozy cried.

"I've got until 9:45 pm, baby girl." Mamie held up the red bulb. "I'm gonna turn the pool lilac."

"Yay!" Cozy jumped up and down.

Mamie clutched the light to her chest, took a deep breath and gracefully jumped feet first into the water. Her platinum locks fanned up like a peacock's tail as she descended, then down again as she pushed off the bottom and shimmied up the pool wall to unscrew the bulb.

Up top, Cozy held her breath in expectation. The pool went dark for a moment before turning lilac. Cozy squealed, clapping, as Mamie swam to the shallow end.

"I wish I could swim like her. Or even swim at all without freaking out," Cozy said.

"Allow me to buy you lessons," Jun-ho said.

"Really?"

He nodded and smiled. She kissed him on the cheek.

"Get ready for the magic," Yeong-jin said, flipping on the Animated Stars Laser Lights. Hundreds of colorful stars whirled across walls, doors, trees, Vic's window . . .

***

A spate of star lights hit Vic's peeping eyes and he nearly tripped over the vacuum cleaner in his leap away from the window. Despite his guilty reaction, this was the first time in forever that his voyeurism was not about stroking king cobra. He wanted preview of the magical decor that would serve as a backdrop for his burgeoning romance, and a memory he and Tanya would recollect on each anniversary celebrating their first kiss. If she came. God, he hoped she'd come. "I'll make her come all right," he said to Number One, who wasn't even there but cowering in the bedroom due to the presence of the dreaded vacuum cleaner.

Vic gauged his progress: living room, vacuumed and dusted; cereal bowls, cleaned and in the cupboard; bed linens, fresh; himself, scrubbed and stuffed into skinny jeans; extruding nose and ear hairs, eradicated. Proto still looked gross, so Vic put it in a new black leather glove and altered a linen jacket to lengthen the right sleeve. The glove would still be visible, but a bit of subtle obfuscation might delay the inevitable what-the-hell-is-wrong-with-you conversation.

A glance at *Killing It* told him his next task was *albums*, as in which vinyl would be placed in full view, partial view, or entirely hidden, and which might best accompany their eventual sexy-time.

***

Tanya used the top of her towel turban to wipe steam off the bathroom mirror. Upon encountering her freshly scrubbed reflection, she zeroed in on her cheekbone, where something misshapen was ripening—a cystic zit, the likes of which she hadn't seen in a decade. Even if she were to pinch out the pus, it would leave behind a messy hole that no manner of concealer could keep from weeping down her cheek. She poked at it with a Q-Tip until her eyes watered. "Yay for me."

***

Proto, perhaps keying into Vic's mounting anxiety and excitement, became a perfect pain in the ass during the LP curation. What the hell did it know about *The Button-Down Mind of Bob Newhart*? That comedy album was over 60 years old. And why did Proto keep placing it in front of the stack? If memory-tapping was the new next step, then it must know Vic owned every Newhart album, movie and TV show ever made. Bob had been Paps's favorite comedian in the world and one of the many gifts he left behind for Vic. Did Proto see the album, then sift through Vic's memories to make a correlation? Or was it simply attracted to the multiple colorful images of Bob on the cover?

In any case, no way was it a front-display record. Miles Davis's *Sketches of Spain* went up front. Then, The Bee Gees's *Saturday Night Fever*. Its vinyl was already loaded on the turntable, ready to drop when Miles finished.

New idea!

He thumbed through the stack of albums, shaking Proto away every time it went back to Newhart, until he found Martin Denny's *Quiet Village*. Pure mid-century exotica. He re-jiggered the albums: first, setting the mood with jungle noises and vibes; second, some Miles for foreplay; third, disco for doin' it.

***

Tanya finished make-up application with a mound of heavy cream foundation she patted gently around the monster zit, which she named "Mr. Hyde."

Mr. Hyde would likely hatch tonight, goddammit.

***

The *Killing It* app scrolled to the next task: cologne application, which Vic had down to a science. Truth be told, Vic felt a little bad for the losers who slathered themselves in Drakkar Noir, sometimes without even washing up after a day of eating someone else's shit. Those guys were decidedly not killing it, nor would they ever be.

For Vic, successful cologne application was one part time, two parts amount, three parts area. Smelling as if you just applied cologne as an afterthought wasn't a good look, so Vic began the application process a minimum of 45 minutes prior to a date. Any earlier, and he risked cologne dissipation, but 45 minutes was optimal for creating a heady combo of factory-made and man-made musk. This way, the pheromones got their fair share. No more than three spritzes sprayed into the air above him. Vic would then wave a hand through the air and dab behind his ears, across his chest, and inches above his you-know-what. If Tanya leaned in to rest her head on his chest during a hug or if things got cooking, she'd catch a little whiff of the good stuff.

He walked into his bathroom; selected a fragrance. Fought the desire to put on Newhart so he could listen while he worked. "You bastard," he yelled at Proto, "you put that in my head." And, as he had the terrible thought that this Bob Newhart incident might be a Singularity, Proto had already squirted Eternity by Calvin Klein into his jeans. "Too much! Belay!" Vic ordered. Proto stopped, placed the bottle back on the counter. "Now I have to air out, you shit." Lefty unzipped the pants. "Bring on the meat," Vic said by rote.

Vic chased a pain med with a slug of Amstel light. The microwave clock said it was 6:55; the music and voices downstairs said the party was in full swing.

She's not coming, he predicted. A sharp bark reminded him of his duties. "All right, Number One." He grabbed the leash.

La Villa Armada was an oasis of strobing lights in a desert of dark buildings flanking the palm tree-lined avenue. Lights beaming above its roof gave the effect of a magical churning cauldron.

Vic and Proto trotted downstairs, winding through arriving party guests. Vic knew he looked dashing in the pastel linen jacket. His hair, impeccable. Crotch smelling of cedar and sandalwood. Damn, he was ready, but nowhere to go except on a poop run. He waved at the sisters, appreciating the big hair bouncing to the beats.

***

Parked halfway down the block, Tanya squirted breath spray, then flipped down the visor. Its lighted mirror showcased the bigger, pointier zit, a volcano with an acidic abyss already liquifying the concealer. She stretched a pin curl over it, then adjusted her bra. *Lift and separate, ladies.*

***

Outside the gate on a rectangle of grass, Number One began his dog poop dance: an elliptical path of indecision and false starts. "Is there really an exact right spot?" Vic asked the mutt who paused, then decided against a spot and resumed his orbit. Vic sang: "Oh-Oh-Oh Number One, you can go number two, oh yes you can, I believe in you." And, on cue, Number One code-browned.

Not 20 feet away, Tanya paused, frozen in the shadow created by a streetlight and palm tree. She held a big bowl covered in plastic wrap. The breeze fluttered her dress as she witnessed the timeless interaction between man and dog.

"Congratulations to you on the number two," Vic sang, shoving Proto inside a clean poop baggie to scoop up the goods. However, when drawing near to the steamy pile, Proto froze in place. Vic tried to push forward, but it wouldn't budge. His mental commands failed. Proto remained immobile. "Do as I comm—!" He cut short at the clacking of Tanya's approaching heels. He pulled the bag off Proto, switched it to Lefty, and by the time she was two feet out, the number two was in a bag.

"Congratulations on a successful mission," Tanya said. Vic nearly gasped at the pin curls and deep red dress—*oh goddess, you are perfumed by roses*—opting for an idiotic chortle. "Hi! You showed up. Uh, this is Number One, Number One, Tanya."

"Hi cutie." Number One rose up like a meerkat to greet her and sniff the bowl. "He's adorable."

"And he knows it. Whatever did you bring us?"

Tanya extended the bowl for his perusal. Vic hid a frown at the massive green clump under the plastic. "It's Grammy's Lime Jell-O Marshmallow Salad, but the gelatin is mixed with vodka instead of water."

"Mmmm." His gaze shifted from the Jell-O to her. "Smells yummy."

Tanya blushed. "Well, it's good and it gets the job done."

Vic resisted speculating about what kind of job they'd get done tonight as he escorted her into La Villa Armada.

19.
THE PARTY DOWNSTAIRS

LASER STARS SPLASHED across drinking and/or dancing people, including Vic and Tanya cutting a Jell-O-shot fueled rug by the pool. The longer sleeve on Vic's jacket didn't hide the leather-clad phalanges as they found excuses to brush against Tanya's hibiscus tattoo.

Tanya caught a few glimpses of it as she swung her head. *Of course*, she thought, *we're still going to play hide-and-seek*, which reminded her of her zit. She turned enough to do a quick, covert pin-curl check.

Mamie cut a path through the dancers, holding her margarita glass high as she approached them. Tanya saw her coming and tapped Vic on the shoulder. Misinterpreting her intent, Vic twirled her silly.

"Hi people, thank you for coming," Mamie yelled over the music. Tanya stopped spinning, but everything around her continued to do so.

"Happy birthday, Cozy!" Vic gave her a side-hug and an air kiss.

"I'm Mamie."

Vic winced. "Shoot, I'm sorry."

"No big, hon. But it is my birthday."

"I should've—"

"Who's this honey?" She eyed Tanya, now swaying from foot to foot.

"I'm Tanya, brilliant party, happy birthday." She flashed Mamie a green-toothed smile.

Mamie pulled her so close Tanya smelled her tequila breath. She danced Tanya around so they both faced Vic, who stopped his meager attempts at keeping the dance alive, and simply stood there, ready to take whatever came. "See this guy? This guy, this is a good guy. He's a hero, this guy," Mamie said.

"Ah, Mamie, you don't need to . . . " Vic began, but Mamie shushed him.

"This guy saved my sister Cozy from drowning. Drowning! She's afraid to swim but she's gonna re-learn, yes, she will. Anyhoo—'back to the facts, ma'am'—her life vest had, um, deflated? And this guy hears her cries. I'm shopping over at Target, so I have no clue what's happening. But this guy jumped into the pool—from the second floor he jumped—and he pulled Cozy to safety. Amen."

"Amen," Tanya agreed.

"That story is 75 percent lies," Vic said, face burning at being in the crosshairs of two drunk women.

"Nah." Mamie swayed in her flip-flops as she gulped her margarita. "All right. But this guy threw the life preserver and dragged her back to the shallow end. So, he did save her." She bowed her head to him. "Thanks, honey." She did the same to Tanya. "Thanks for coming honey."

"Nice to meet you."

Vic and Tanya watched Mamie boogie away through the crow, then regarded one another, each holding a different idea of what this moment meant. Vic leaned into her slow and sexy. Tanya veered away and shouted in his ear: "Imagine someone telling a story that's only 25 percent true. Can you imagine?"

"What did I do?"

Tanya reached out to the crook of his V-neck t-shirt and flicked his dog tag. "Did you buy this at The Supply Sergeant?"

"No, it's real. What? Oh, you were referring to my story from our first . . . ?"

She stared at him. Duh, yes.

"I was an IT guy. Our convoy drove very close to a skirmish, a deadly skirmish. Gunfire echoed off the mountains. It sounded close. We thought we were being ambushed. Thankfully, we weren't. And I guess I embellished it. I didn't know you."

"So you only lie to strangers?"

"Now I'm telling the truth." Vic tried to soul-gaze her, but she wouldn't play.

"As a side-note: I prefer Superman to Lex Luther."

"Understood."

Tanya couldn't decide about this guy. If she overlooked all the peculiarities and mystery and chose the romantic route, put in the time, helped him become an actual man, he would undoubtedly share the newer, better Him with a different Her, and Tanya would be cast aside. It was not unprecedented. *Plus, he lies*.

"How about telling your story on the record?" she said.

"Well, I'm developing this app, and any negative publicity—"

"It's already part of a listicle. Readers are clamoring for more, for the whole truth." *Readers. Clamoring. Heh.* Well, it wasn't a total lie because she was a reader, and she was clamoring.

"There's an article?"

"Your hospital visit is public record."

"I thought that stuff was confidential."

"Unless the police get involved. You weren't identified by name."

"Police?"

"Apparently, you ran through the restaurant parking lot, tore off a windshield wiper and tried to beat off the parking attendant." *Oops.* "You know what I mean."

"I know what you mean, but I don't remember doing it." As he spoke, a memory flashed: Norman and a cop jostling him into the Subaru and Vic conking his head on the baby seat.

Tanya made a pleading face. "I only need the barest of details and a few quotes."

"Why don't we discuss it upstairs?"

Tanya hesitated, then nodded. "I'll get the rest of Grammy's Jell-O." She weaved through the crowd to a table filled with empty plastic margarita glasses and the bowl, still a third full.

Vic whistled for Number One, who sprang off someone's lap and followed them upstairs.

"Want to see me recreate my life-saving dive?" Vic pretended he was going to jump over the railing. She laughed, shaking her head "no" as he led her inside his apartment.

20.
THE PARTY UPSTAIRS

"QUIET VILLAGE"** played as Tanya and her bowl of Jell-O inspected his abode, beginning with the record display. "Why are parrots screaming at us?"

"Oh . . . the music will get . . . should I change it?" Tanya grinned and shook her head, moving to the oil paintings. "That's *A Boy and his Dog*," Vic said.

"Is that what the symbols say?" She squinted at the Japanese characters. "Or are you just describing what I'm seeing?"

"Ha, no, that's how it translates. The other is *Birds and a Maiden*."

"Pretty."

"And *Lovers in a Garden*." Vic noticed that she barely gave it a glance. *What's she trying to tell me? It's not as if I took her on the tour, ending with The Bedroom, dot-dot-dot.*

She stopped at the Hoo Maru painting, taking in the mighty frigate, the stormy sea, a spoonful of Jell-O. "This I love, truly." Behind her, Vic-tory pumped the air.

She moved to the sword display. "I didn't know I'd hoped you'd have these until this very second." Her words had thickened to a slur.

"They're recreations of feudal Japanese swords," Vic explained. "I practice the art of Kendo."

"Right. I remember you telling me." She reached up to stroke the shaft of a wood bokuto, also sneaking a quick armpit sniff.

"I remember how you looked in the candlelight," he said, and immediately regretted it during the silence that followed. Man and woman on either side of the room—he, mired in the embarrassment of sounding like a weirdo who falls in love too fast, while she was halfway between tipsy and blotto, readying to tell him something she thought he needed to know.

"Before you say something else, I used to date this brilliant poet . . . " She licked her spoon clean. " . . . I was crazy with a K about him. I mean, I once attacked a woman with a broken beer bottle. Smashed it on the edge of a table because he flirted with her. I would have considered self-immolation if he'd asked nice enough." She handed Vic her empty bowl. "As it turned out, he was just a purposefully unmedicated bipolar narcissistic a-hole who wore make-up and lived in his car."

"He was homeless?"

"No, he lived in his car."

"I'm not on medication aside from CoQ10, fish oil and ginseng—"

"What I'm getting to is that you should take off the glove, Vic."

He saw this coming, but hadn't formulated an explanation, so winged it: "Some people have wounds on the outside and other people have them on the inside." He fought to keep Proto stuffed in his pocket, continuing, "Those are the fortunate ones who can conceal the wound until a time when mutual trust develops, and they feel comfortable confiding in another person."

"And you don't feel comfortable confiding in me?"

Shit. How to answer that question? It wasn't a matter of distrust; it was more about her rejecting him for his malady. "If I take off the glove, what'll you take off?"

"Oh, I don't know, my disapproving frown?"

Consigned to his fate, Vic sat close but not too close to her, and began a burlesque of pulling off the glove in sync with the music.

Tanya struggled with patience. *Tick-tock, jerkoff.*

With a last tug, the glove pulled free. Tanya swallowed a gasp at the perfectly normal thumb welded to an icky skin graft.

"It's a prosthesis that's merging with the arm. The skin will . . . it'll look real at some point."

Tanya requested permission with her eyes. Vic nodded. She reached out to Proto, who met her halfway. Their palms touched.

"I thought all I needed was a little hydrogen peroxide," Vic explained. "The whole thing from beginning to . . . the incident . . . happened in two days."

"What thing, exactly, happened in two days?" she asked, extricating her hand from Proto, who briefly held on before letting go.

"I lost most of the hand is all I can say right now. Kept the thumb, as you can see. But it's weak."

"And during all this you go out on a date?"

"Some things are worth it."

"Yeah, I'm worth your hand."

"Four fingers and half the palm, technically."

"May I take a picture of the"—*creature*— "prosthesis?"

"Proto . . . is what we call it."

She pulled out her cell. "It's super cool," she lied. Vic's face brightened. "Can you hold a sword?"

"Yes!" Vic galloped over to his display. Lefty got the blade, Proto got a bokuto.

"Maybe take off the jacket?" Vic tore off his jacket. Tanya adjusted a lamp for more light. Vic assumed a pose showcasing each hand and katana.

Tanya focused the camera close enough on Proto to show contrast between sleek sword texture and the hand's surface-of-the-moon quality, took a few shots, then switched over to video and pressed record. "Victor, when did you first suspect something was wrong?"

"Oh, wait, I have better pants!" Vic skipped out of the living room.

Tanya paused the recording and rubbed her temples feeling the headache to come. She tottered over to Vic's bookshelf, noting the extensive collection of *Star Trek* books, a dozen graphic novels from every genre, *On the Road*—of course—a few Gaiman's and Bukowski's—ditto *and ditto*—then turned her attention to a group of framed photos on the top shelf.

The first showed a teenaged Vic and an old man whom he resembled posed together in matching red *Star Trek* shirts. Another was a publicity photo of a handsome bearded man in a black and red uniform. She squinted at the felt tip writing at the bottom: *Dear Vic & Paps, "The more difficult the task, the sweeter the victory!" Stay icy! J. Frakes ("Lt. Riker) ("Number One)!"* That explained the dog's name.

The last was also the saddest. A framed funeral announcement for Waltham "Paps" Moss. The birth and death dates told her he died about two years ago at age 91. The faded image of a young Paps in an army uniform looked nearly identical to Vic.

Fuzziness and guilt and a soaring inebriation filled her as she scrolled her phone, stopping on the close-up shot of Vic's curious appendage gripping the sword handle. The image that'll bait thousands of clicks. Though knowing very little about any *Star Trek* iterations prior to the 21st century, for some reason she thought, *set to stun*.

"I'm wearing my lucky pants, my lucky pants," Vic sang, trouncing into the living room, shirtless and wearing flowing black pants. "Whenever I wear my lucky pants, I gotta do a crazy dance—"

Tanya lunged, a ferocious kissing beast. Vic smooched back. Proto touched her waist, slid up her rib cage, and clambered over her shoulder to stroke the tattoo.

They pulled apart to gulp for air.

"I don't live in my car and you already know all my secrets," Vic whispered huskily, followed by more face-sucking. Number One scooted out of their way as they flopped down on the couch, pressing into each other urgently. Tanya sat up to unzip her dress. Vic bolted to the stereo and put on *Saturday Night Fever*.

"I'm gonna rock your world, bitch-boy," Tanya called from the couch.

Yes, yes, yes! The driving beat of "Stayin Alive" began; Vic shook his ass at her, strutted backwards, lips pursed in an Elvis pout. "I'm a dancin' man!" He spun Travolta-style to . . . Tanya, nestled into the couch cushions. Green-lipped, messy-haired, unconscious.

"What? What?" Vic cried. "Tanya?" She mumbled incoherently. "Nooooooo." He stood staring at her for a moment. She was out. "Damn."

Vic sighed and hoisted her legs up on the couch, rolled her on her side, sliding the Japanese neck pillow under her head. Proto slithered out for a last rub of the tat. "Belay!" Vic whisper-yelled. Proto obeyed, helped Lefty tuck the blanket under her chin. Vic ran into the kitchen for a glass of water, which he placed on the trunk. All set.

He extracted the cell phone from her hand, accidentally swiped it active. And there it was: the image of Proto. *Fuck*. He knew she wanted him for a story, but this horror-show close-up seemed exploitative. He hit the back arrow and raised the camera to her, moving closer to capture her gigantic zit, a ripe white head at its tip. *How would you like it?*

He considered leaving the image to humiliate her tomorrow. She'd obviously attempted to hide it with make-up; probably didn't want it exploited. Maybe she'd learn a lesson. He shook his head. *I'm not that guy,* he thought, erasing the image. He considered also deleting the Proto picture, but 86'd the idea, because, well, because she kissed him. And there was hope yet. So he dropped the phone on the couch, shut off music and lights, and whistled for Number One to follow him to bed. As boy and dog retired, Vic decided he'd surprise her with pancakes in the morning.

21.

SEPARATION

DOZENS OF PLASTIC margarita cups twinkled in the pool as the sun rose over La Villa Armada. Somewhere up in the nearby foothills, a rooster crowed.

In Vic's living room, conscious/unconscious Vic Moss had questions: *Why am I naked in the living room? Why do I stand over her? Proto, what are you touching? What the fuck are you holding in your—? Belay, you bastard! Move away from my—Wait! Don't move. Keep it cupped.*

Tanya's eyes opened. She sprung off the couch. "What is—? What are you doing? Oh God—" A wrong turn into the coffee table trunk sent her tumbling to the floor.

In the next moment Vic became fully conscious and found himself naked and looming over her. Proto cupped his dick and balls. "Oh no!"

"Where's my purse?" She stumbled to her feet, hair flying wild, same as her eyes. "Where's my fucking purse?"

"I must have been sleepwalking!"

"Shoes first, shoes, shoes, shoes . . . " She reeled around, found them, grabbed them. "Purse, purse, purse . . . " She circled the couch as Vic lurched after her, issuing a torrent of explanations.

"I don't know how—I had no bad intentions. I was covering my privates, so the intention was I don't know, to get some cereal, which I do every morning, usually naked."

"Why am I so stupid?"

"I was probably being discreet, or maybe I forgot you were here!"

Tanya found her purse by the stereo. "Purse!"

"I mean, you passed out, so I put a blanket on you and went to my room—"

"I never should have even come here last night—"

"—Number One is my witness!"

She flung the blanket off the couch, pulled out the cushions. "Keys, keys, keys . . . "

"I swear to you right here and now, I'm not this guy, please, Tanya!" Proto reached out, entreating forgiveness, but Vic barked him down, "Belay! *Belay* you motherfucker!"

Tanya stopped her frantic spinning, hysteria supplanted by an icy calm. "Pardon me?"

"No, no, no, not you. I was talking to—" He pointed to Proto, still cupping his gentlemen.

"Oh, what a relief, you were talking to your special hand. Gee, I feel so much better." She slipped into her pumps, stopped to gulp water.

"I don't want you to leave this way!"

"What way, Victor? Vicky? Vic the Tic? How am I leaving? Please articulate."

"Pissed?"

"You're *still naked!*"

"Gah!" He streaked to the bedroom. Number One followed him, yipping frantically.

Tanya shook her purse, heard the jangle of keys. "Of course." Steadying her breathing, she marched to the door, flipped the lock on the door handle but the door didn't open. "Open, open!" She tried flipping the deadbolt. It wouldn't give. She dropped her purse to pound on the door with both fists. "Open, open, open!"

"Let me . . . " Vic ran out to her rescue. "You have to jiggle it . . . " He clicked it open.

"For fuck's sake, why would you put on a t-shirt before pants? What kind of person are you?"

Vic looked down at his uncupped cock, flaccid, yet peekaboo-ing out beyond the t-shirt. Proto was holding a pair of jeans. "Oh no."

Tanya flew outside. On her way downstairs she came up with the title for the MyDiary entry on this: "Naked Monster Woke Me Up."

***

Mamie opened her door across the way. "Hon, come look at this." Cozy appeared beside her, handed her a cup of coffee. They watched Vic emerge from his place still buttoning his jeans, and in hot pursuit of the fleeing woman, who was now shaking the stuck gate.

"We should get that fixed," Mamie said.

Cozy nodded. "I'll call Felix."

Vic reached out to the woman, and although the sisters couldn't hear words, the tone was pleading.

"Tanya. That's her name," said Mamie.

Tanya pepper sprayed him. He yowled like a monkey in a bear trap, clutching his eyes as she muscled the gate open and fled.

"Should we do something?" said Cozy.

"What? Get the hose out?"

Both cinched their matching frilly robes and moved to the railing.

***

Vic staggered up the stairs, a wounded Frankenstein. He paused at his door to rub his eyes—with Lefty—and inhale the cool, dry morning air, oblivious to the many witnesses around him . . . behind parted blinds and through doors open as far as their chains allowed.

"Everything okay, hon?" Mamie called.

Vic smiled through a stream of tears. "All good, just a misunderstanding."

Mamie shrugged and returned to her apartment. Cozy hesitated. "All right, let us know if you need anything."

"Thanks." He waited until their door closed, then ran inside to his kitchen, where he wetted a hand towel and pressed it over his eyes. He emptied his mind of everything but positive imagery of Proto and Lefty wielding the swords as a team. There would be no negative thoughts for Proto to act on. He ignored Number One's wet nose pushing at his ankles, his mind brimming with their copasetic sword routine. Such harmony between man and robot hand. *So much power together,* Vic thought. *Right, Proto?*

Proto didn't respond.

He raised Proto for a man-to-hand confab. "Let's not lie to each other. This was a setback, and I'm pretty sure it was your fault. You didn't understand the rules. That's okay. It's nothing we can't fix together."

Still nothing from Proto, not even a twitch.

"Aw come on, pal. Listen up. The best way to wind down, in this guy's opinion, is a routine, ya know? So . . . let's do the 14-angle form again."

Vic headed to the katana display. Proto accepted the bokuto after a brief hesitation. Lefty took the bladed sword. "Okay, let's warm up the wrists." Lefty and Proto rotated their swords in figure-eights.

"Ki-ken-tai-ichi." Vic's mind remained on the routine to come. "All right, let's take first position." Proto performed a forward thrusting strike. "Good job!" Vic navigated toward the coffee trunk, keeping his mind blank. "Okay, let's do positions two and three." High horizontal strikes to the right and left. "Looking good. Now four and five." Diagonal down strikes, right, then left. "Great work! Let's go back to first position." Proto repeated the forward thrusting strike, arm straight out in front of Vic.

FLUMP! Vic slammed Proto onto the trunk.

Lightning-fast Lefty struck, hacking the blade into its wrist. Blistering pain spiderwebbed throughout Vic's body. He howled. Pink blood spouted. Number One yapped, hysterically scampering into the kitchen. The more Proto flopped around, the more blood squirted everywhere. Vic bit his lip, withdrew the blade from the wound, cocked back for another strike. But Proto charged, punching him in the nose—once, twice. Vic pitched backward into the bookshelf. Everything came off its shelves. Glass broke. A flashflood of blood and snot threatened to drown him. Still, he bellowed to shake the walls: "I'm going to murder you!"

Proto stabbed at his eyes with its new, pointed nails. Vic ducked too late. The middle nail hooked him in the tear duct, shredding a thin slice down the side of his nose to his chin. The skin flapped open, expulsing blood and cheek meat.

"Get off, get off!" His mind fired orders to Proto: *move away from the face! Pull off!* But by now, Proto's index and middle fingers had latched onto his eyelashes. "Get the fuck off!" He couldn't use the sword or he'd cut off his own head!

Proto sliced his eyelid fold and ripped the lid clear off, exposing the naked cornea, and with that, Vic's *full fucking fury*. He bit into the forefinger, crunching "skin" and "veins." Proto spasmed. Vic thwacked Proto down onto the trunk again and raised the sword. "*Die, die, die!*"

In the split-second Vic took to blink blood from his eyes, Proto clamped nails down on the wooden ridges of the trunk for leverage and heaved itself in the opposite direction of the wrist, that carbon-based pussy flesh! Proto pulled away from the rest of Vic with the force of a freight train. Vic squawked, dropped the sword as fuzzy white light infiltrated his peripheral vision. Faux flesh and actual flesh separated. Licks of fire shot up Vic's arm, pinballing around in his skull. Tendons snapped, bone and machine avulsed, arteries exploded.

Proto hopped off the trunk just as Vic collapsed onto it with a wet smack. Shock struck him paralyzed. He watched Proto attack the thumb, severing most of the connective tissues before giving up and dragging it by flimsy strands towards the bedroom, leaving behind a snail's trail of blood clots.

Vic would have bled out had the front door not opened

and the sisters raced in. Somewhere in the middle of their ingress, everything slowed to half speed. The sisters' faces gradually contorted into terror as they saw Vic's damage. Words were stripped of everything but languid bass tones. In sloth-speed, Cozy pulled off her robe and plugged the blood spout. Mamie fumbled with her phone, so slowly it seemed like a levitation.

Vic heard himself yell, "I can't afford an ambulance!"

Then all sounds merged into the CLICK of the bedroom door shutting.

***

In a car, in yet another back seat. Music.

Mamie drove. Cozy turned around from the passenger seat to trickle water into Vic's mouth and then over the lidless eye. The robe wrapped around his stump was soaked in blood, as was the robe he had pressed onto his split-open face.

"Please take care of Number One," he told her in a weak croak.

On Cozy's bewildered look, Mamie chimed in, "He means his dog, hon." She adjusted the rearview mirror so she could see him, with his giant unblinking eye and torn-up mug.

"Of course we will, hon," Cozy said.

At that, Vic's single eyelid fluttered. Cozy's crispy skin and cleavage were the last things he saw before the world whited out.

22.
5150

FROM A TWO-MILE and closing distance, the coastline was a hobbyist's miniature with a tiny line of hotels and palm trees and itty-bitty people gathered on its white sand beach. The shadow of a 100-foot wave sent the beach patrons scattering as it rumbled nearer. Vic crested the wave. He didn't need no stinking surfboard because he was the top-ranked foot surfer, which was a thing, at least in Schedule II narcotic hospital drug dreams. His feet and arms danced for balance, but the turbulent wind lashed him, and he teetered, then slid down the wave's 90-degree wall into the trough. The wave steamrolled south, crashing over him in an explosion of foam. Vic, now somehow encased in a plastic bubble, enjoyed the tumult. A passing fish! A sharp rock outcropping! Its jagged peak punctured the bubble, exposing Vic to a frenzied 360-degree spin that whomped him into a hospital bed.

Holy shit! The big orderly was giving him a sponge bath. What man or beast could wake up to a non-consensual ass-wiping without a wail of indignation? So wail he did. And fight and kick and squirm.

But Eddie had wrestled his way into college, so restraining this skinny jag offered no challenge. He always began with the ass, just to get it out of the way.

***

Normally, when a class ended, Tanya basked in a post-Kundalini bliss better than any drink or drug. Today she fretted over the whereabouts of her phone. With her friend—and Kundalini employer—Crystal's phone tucked into her neck, Tanya fetched a real-life miniature gong from the candles shelf.

She bent over Mr. Lake, who was sleeping peacefully under a blanket of his own farts and banged the little wicker mallet on the gong once, twice.

Mr. Lake snorted, opened his eyes. A big smile broke through a landscape of wrinkles. "Great class, Tammy." He popped to his feet to roll up his mat. Kundalini was his religious experience, and Mr. Lake experienced it fully. She admired his lack of shame. How many classes had she not benefited from Kundalini's healing properties because she was too busy suppressing flatulence?

A computer voice on the phone said: "Hello, Crystal Jackson-Murphy."

"No, I'm Tanya R. Lazonga, calling from her—"

"Hello, Crystal Jackson-Murphy—"

"No, she's—" Tanya shot a look at the real Crystal Jackson-Murphy leading Mr. Lake to the door. "Human being please. I want to talk to a human."

"Please choose from the following options—"

"Stop. Human. Human. Human."

"You said you want to talk to a representative, is that right?"

"Yes."

"Please hold while we find someone to help you."

Crystal zipped through the studio spraying air freshener. Tanya waved it away and headed to the door. "Pumpkin spice, really?"

"Tis the season," Crystal said.

"It's barely September!" Tanya opened the door, gulping a lung-full of fresh air, well . . . hot, dry air with a hint of smog.

A real human voice spoke to her. "Hi, am I speaking to Crystal Murphy?"

"No, I'm using her phone. I lost my phone."

"Hello? Crystal Murphy?"

"Am I speaking to a human?"

"Hello?"

The call terminated. "Shoot!" Tanya stomped around in frustration. "I don't want to do this again!"

"Where did you last see it? That always helps me," said Crystal.

Tanya knew where she last saw the phone. But how to explain the very good date followed by the very bad morning where a frenzied escape had resulted in a team member left behind? Seemed easier to buy a new phone. "Maybe it fell into a storm drain," she said.

"You know what you should do? You should call yourself," Crystal said.

***

After another round of painkillers and some warm broth, Vic answered a phone that didn't belong to him, courtesy of the sisters, who'd brought a few things from home, and mistakenly included Tanya's—but not his—phone.

A few minutes later he was explaining his second favorite Hemingway novel. " . . . 'bout this guy who loved a lady but got his junk blown off in the war so their love could never be consummated, and they both went insane."

"Again, Vic, which hospital? Memorial?" Tanya asked for the fifth time.

"I think so."

"Can you give my phone to Eddie? He's the big orderly with the dragon on his neck?"

"He gave me a bath."

"Good, then you know him."

"I wanna know you . . . " Things got foggy fast. The phone slid onto Vic's pillow; Tanya's voice grew faint. Eyes fluttering, Vic reached deep for strength, rearing back and rolling the good half of his face onto the phone.

" . . . I think separate paths are the way to go for us,"

Tanya was saying. "Or a single path, but in opposite directions. Or the same direction but at different times."

"Are you breaking up with me!" he screamed into the pillow.

"We were never a thing. I wanted a story. You wanted to stand over me while I slept, holding your penis."

Vic felt the pull of another gathering wave yet managed to raise his lips off the pillow. "I swear to God I just wanted cereal . . . " but the wave surged, and he lost track of the conversation, specifically, of how it ended. But it did end. Gravity sucked him down the wave wall, where he hung for a moment like Wile E. Coyote, acknowledging the crushing plunge about to befall him; in this moment came the sound of someone clearing his throat, which directed Vic's attention to a man in a suit in the guest chair.

"I already got a bath," Vic told him.

The man's chuckle rattled with phlegm. "Oh, Mr. Moss, we're going to have to dial down the meds a little, aren't we? I'll tell a gal." He made a note in the file folder in his lap.

Discombobulated from having fallen asleep during one conversation and waking up in the middle of another, Vic could only look at the dude, then to the folder, then back to the dude.

"Before the phone call," the Suit said in the measured voice of a bored bureaucrat, "I was explaining the three-day observation period we are legally required to impose if someone becomes a threat to himself or others."

"Have you checked the bedroom? It's in the bedroom."

"We searched the apartment, Mr. Moss."

"It's fucking hiding from you! Why won't anybody believe me?"

The Suit's eyes remained neutral as he listened to Vic recount the story he'd been selling since entering the ER yesterday about an evil hand prosthesis that had done something bad and was hiding in his bedroom.

Vic's rambling slowed until he fell silent.

"You're only moving two floors upstairs. 72 hours only, in which time we'll figure all of this out and . . . " The patient was asleep. The Suit closed Vic's file, slipping it under another file labeled "Henry Hatch," who had torn out his own eye last week. The police suspected Henry consumed the eye, and then somehow cauterized the wound. Two similar cases in a week. The Suit blamed civilization. Some folks couldn't hack living in the End Times.

Eddie entered, helped Vic onto a wheelchair. The Suit tossed the folders onto Vic's blanketed legs and stepped aside so Eddie could wheel him out.

As he rolled Vic along the corridor, Eddie flicked a looksee behind him. The old guy was ten feet behind, far enough he wouldn't see Eddie snooping through the folders.

***

In a different bed with the curtains drawn around him, in a more sober state, Vic stuffed his ears with Kleenex to mute the whimpering of an unseen roommate on the other side of the curtain.

Vic learned several things during his stay. He was going to have a gnarly scar. At first glance in the nurse's hand mirror, he'd almost vomited at the sight of a dozen staples snaking down his face where Proto had split him open like a pomegranate. Also, eyes have two eyelids. Never had he considered the lower lid, only those few times in his early club-kid days when he'd dusted a hint of shadow on it to make his eyes pop.

He also faced two choices going forward: forever wear a gel pad on the eyeball so it stays moist and secure an eyepatch on top to keep it in place—or pay the outrageous deductible and get another prosthetic, from reputable doctors.

What he couldn't or wouldn't face was two strikes were out for Tanya, choosing instead to believe that *a noble act might rouse milady*. He held up her phone and snapped a close-up of his newly bandaged stump with no thumb. *Does she need to see the face, too?* He kept his eyes out of the shot, in case her promise of anonymity was bullshit.

His tolerance of the continued whimpering on the other side of the curtain faded. All that pitiful clamoring sent Vic on his own journey of self-pity, visiting his mom who ran off; his MIA alcoholic dick of a dad; Grandma who died when he was a baby; and Paps, who was no more. Nobody to worry about him. Well, Norman came to visit, brought his kid, talked to him like he was five. He'd add that in the "Positive Thoughts" area on *Killing It*—"I have, Norman."

Eddie the Orderly entered the room on a mission. His lady reporter had texted and so he was now earning his future cookies and cigarette.

"I already had a bath!" Vic cringed in Eddie's shadow.

"No tipo, I'm here for the phone."

Vic handed it over, relieved. "Could you get a full-length shot for her before you go?"

"Sure." Eddie backed away as far as he could, holding the phone vertically.

"Not my face!" Vic cried, pulling a pillow over his head, then issuing a muffled "Okay, ready."

Eddie took a few with the flash on, then off. "You're getting outta here tomorrow morning."

Under the pillow, Vic nodded, happy at the news. He sure hoped Number One was okay, and the hand wasn't . . . hunting him. Oh God, would it do that?

23.
CLEAN-UP

AFTER THIS SHITSHOW, I'm going to watch a movie, drink some wine, smoke some weed; I'm not in the mood for sex tonight," Mamie said, her Bluetooth earbuds winking as she strolled over to Vic's place.

Cozy followed with a mop and bucket, a dust-buster, plastic gloves, and rolls of paper towels tucked under her arms. Rambo the Maid.

"All right, cute stuff," Mamie said. "I mean, who knows, maybe I'll need it later . . . " She fumbled with the keys. "Shrimp sounds good." She made a kissing sound. "Annyeonghi gyeseyo." She clicked off and opened the door.

A man's voice greeted them from the stereo. Bob Newhart's, in fact. " . . . now the advertising people, realizing this, would have had to create a Lincoln. And I think they would have gone about it something like this . . . "

Mamie turned off the stereo. "That must have been playing non-stop."

She joined Cozy in gawking at the pile of soft-serve cheek chunks on the trunk and the blood trail leading to the bedroom.

"I feel so sad, looking at this," Cozy said. "Hey, where's the dog?"

On cue, Number One padded out of the kitchen with

his tail between his legs, and guilt on his cute little face. "Poor baby," Mamie said. She found a small pile of poop on the rug under the kitchen sink. "That's all right, sweetheart, we all shit the rug sometimes." Cozy handed her a paper towel. "Gonna take him out for a spin." She gave the full paper towel back to Cozy to toss and herded Number One to the door.

Cozy dropped the poop into one of the plastic bags she brought, and then inserted her earbuds. Sounds from the outside world were promptly replaced by screaming female punks.

"Hon, I can hear it on the outside! Turn it down!" Mamie said on her way out.

Cozy made no response, but lowered the music, resenting Mamie for compelling her to do so. She used the kitchen sink to fill the bucket, watching the suds rise while brooding about how Mamie always bossed her around. Mamie, who was all of 11 months older but played the mom, who swam like Esther Williams, who got to walk the dog while Cozy had to clean. She went back into the living room and set the bucket down by the mess on the carpet.

Cozy eyed the trunk, riddled with the hodgepodge of yuck, except for a stack of brochures unaffected by whatever the heck went down. She still couldn't figure out the particulars, but the police and hospital people called it a suicide attempt. Maybe because of the girl?

To Cozy, dealing with this was akin to learning to swim. You didn't jump into the deep end. You started at the top step of the shallow end, which was—Cozy looked around—the bookshelf.

She began with the bigger pieces of glass, then let the hand vac eat the smaller shards. She replaced the photos on the top shelf. Paps's funeral announcement had a crack down the middle in the shape of a lightning bolt. *Poor Vic*.

A reflection in the glass made her jump and spin. The bedroom door had opened. By itself! "Hello?" She stood still for a moment, skin tingling. "Oh gosh, oh gosh."

Imagining what Mamie would do, brave Mamie, she tiptoed closer, inches from the door. Sucking in her breath, she leaned forward to peer into the room. Empty. Oh goodness. Such a relief. The blood trail thinned out, stopping altogether at the pile of dirty clothes in the middle of the room. Since the police combed through the room, she assumed there were no hand parts to be found, despite what Vic babbled about when they deposited him in the ER.

***

Mamie waited patiently as Number One turned a 360 on his shitting grass. He chose a spot and assumed position but yielded no bounty. He shot Mamie a hopeless look. "Let's go into nature, Number One." She walked him around the edge of the building, where large bushy oaks surrounded the apartments' backsides, providing the tenants with verdant views from their bedroom windows, and cooling shade in the summer. "That's your house, up there, see?" Mamie said, pointing up at Vic's second-story bedroom window. "Kinda makes a little fella wanna doody, yes?" Mamie wrinkled the waste bag as an auditory cue. "Right? Time to doody?"

Number One sniffed around, did a half-assed circle, and hunkered down to do business when something moved up there on the branch. He rose on his hind legs, howling, paws scrabbling on the oak's trunk.

"It's probably just a squirrel, calm down," said Mamie, cocking her head and squinting up at a branch. She'd had it trimmed so it didn't touch Vic's windowsill. He'd been certain this was a spider bridge. And although he never implicated her and Cozy in his spider tragedy, the sisters still felt bad about neglecting the encroaching foliage.

Number One continued bawling. Mamie raised her phone, zooming in until the window was in close-up. Ah, the screen had fallen and caught in a branch. Other than that, all she saw was the open screenless window. No squirrel. No loitering critters. "Let's go, and then you're gonna go, buster."

***

Cozy found the bedroom window open, and the screen gone. Outside, the oak leaves fluttered in the hot breeze, calm-inducing proof that everything freaky could be explained. The door wasn't closed properly, so wind from the window pushed it open. Simple. She skirted around the laundry, closed the window and then the door behind her.

She used the brochures to scrape bits and dibbles off the trunk into a metal bowl she'd found in the kitchen. Music kept her unaware of the disgusting sounds the viscera made as it *thunked* into the bowl. But another noise cut through just fine—

A *thud*. From the bedroom. She straightened up like a deer hearing a boot crunch, muted her music, cocked her head. Only silence.

"Stop being a baby," she muttered, restarting the music, and grabbing a sponge and bucket to work on the carpet. She began with the muck by the trunk and worked her way towards . . . she knew where this ended.

She'd gotten halfway to the bedroom when she paused to assess her progress. The job so far had nearly abolished the stains, but they'd definitely have to call the maintenance guy to do a steam cleaning. If she were a CSI lady, she'd give more intellectual real estate to the obvious dragging pattern and might surmise something bloody had been dragged into the bedroom.

Another noise. "Jesus!" She removed the earbuds. Someone was in the bedroom. She knew it. She felt it. If the door opened again, Cozy knew she'd lose her mind.

She grabbed the bottle of 409 and got to her feet, taking a few furtive steps closer to the bedroom. And a few more. She leaned in until her ear pressed against the door. Always an empath, Cozy would later swear she sensed an aura from the other side. There was also creaking, as though someone stood on a bad floorboard. A squatter?

"Hello?" Cozy pictured one of those hopping Chinese vampires.

As she backed away, her left flip-flop sank into a wet spot, and wetness oozed over the top and under her foot. "Oh, shoot!" She hopped one-legged to the front door, opened it, and kicked off the sandal.

"Hello to you, too, hon," Mamie said as she and doggie got to the top stair. Number One hot-footed around Cozy and ran inside. Cozy looked stricken. "What's your deal, hon?"

"I . . . I was cleaning. I saw a reflection in the glass . . . " Cozy began, but Mamie was already inside.

"Wowza, good work so far, sis." Mamie eyeballed the clean trunk, the tidy bookshelf and the much-diminished blood trail. "We should still get Felix in here with a power steamer."

Cozy pointed at the bedroom door which was once again ajar. "That door was closed. I swear to God! It was closed. Then it opened by itself! And then I closed it. And I heard a noise! And now it's open, again!"

"Did you check the carpet in the bedroom?" Mamie strolled alongside the light bloodstains. "What the hell happened? Did he drag himself in there? Or the hospital people tracked the blood in . . . ?"

"Listen to me for once in your life, someone is in there," Cozy hissed furiously.

Mamie searched Cozy's panicked face. She wanted to believe her, but the vrooming of motorcycles triggered Cozy. So did trash trucks. Waves crashing. Knives scraping china plates. Thunder. The noises children make on a playgrounds.

Mamie pushed the door open with her nails. "We don't take kindly to squatters in these parts." Number One trotted out, holding something in his mouth.

"What are you eating?" Mamie demanded, reaching for him, but the dog veered around her. Cozy made a grab, but he faked her out and dashed into the kitchen.

"He's eating something," Cozy cried, blocking his path as Mamie closed in.

"Give it, Number One!" Mamie lunged. He ducked aside, but she caught his collar and folded him into a headlock. His paws flapped in vain protest. "Drop it!" Mamie shook him. "Drop it."

Number One's jaw slackened, and out rolled what was left of Vic's thumb: a rotting mushroom with a half-gnawed thumbprint.

"What do we do?" Cozy threw up her hands. "I used all the paper towels."

"It's too late." Mamie set the hand vac to 'turbo' and let the suction do its work.

24.
HOME AGAIN

NORMAN'S SUBARU ROARED away from the hospital pickup curb while Vic was still trying to fasten his seat belt.

His part-time toddler, Hanna, strapped into her baby-seat in the back, wore a tiny version of Norman's Dodgers cap and held a giant foam finger almost as big as she.

Vic finally got his belt latched and turned to her. "Hi, Hanna banana."

Her little brown eyes shot darts of suspicion at his bandaging.

"I lost my hand."

"Dumb ass."

Norman suppressed a grin.

"Say again?"

"Dummy dumb dumbass."

Vic shook his head at Norman. "Real nice."

"Nothing I wouldn't say to your face."

"You've never made a bad decision?"

"I never c-u-t o-f-f m-y h-a-n-d."

"For the hundredth time, I did not cut off the damned thing," Vic spat. "It *tore away* from me, and it took my fuck—my thumb. I almost b-l-e-d out."

"You're having a tough go of it, that's for sure, little buddy."

"That's it? That's all you got, Skipper? No proverbs? No Marianne? No Deepak? No Gandalf?"

Norman looked thoughtful. "Check yo self before you wreck yo self?"

***

Cozy insisted on keeping the dog at their place until Vic returned, so Number One got to crash on a luxury towel on their couch. As for the apartment, they'd tack carpet remediation costs onto Vic's rent, yet still wanted to spend as little as possible, which meant a little more elbow grease before they called Felix. Vic was expected home soon, and Mamie didn't want him tromping across the wet carpet making things worse. So, armed with her most powerful blow dryer and an extension cord, she marched to his place and let herself in. Cozy had begged her not to go inside. Swore there *was* something lurking about. Mamie assured her that the fear was a product of the violent situation they'd borne witness to, and even if something was there, Mamie would beat it to death with the blow dryer.

The stereo was on. Newhart again. "Abe, do this piece the way Charley wrote it, would ya?" Audience laughter. "The inaugural address won, didn't it?" Mamie turned off the stereo and slipped the album back into its cover. Her visit would be short and to the point. No bandwidth or desire to guess why the stereo kept turning itself back on.

She plugged in the extension cord, set the dryer to high heat, then held it a few inches from the damp carpet, beginning at the bedroom door and working her way to the trunk.

Cozy had done a bang-up job. Nobody would know what horror had besmirched the trunk. It was better than new. Except for the cereal bowl wherein a few bloated Captain Crunch balls floated in a puddle of milk. "Where did you come from?"

Mamie opened the bedroom, saw nobody. She kicked the laundry pile before opening the closet, then closed the window she'd swear was already closed. Resisting the urge to draw scary conclusions, she made a mental note to call the Felix about the loose screen.

She peeked into the bathroom, behind the shower curtain, then deposited the cereal bowl in the kitchen, startled by the empty water glass on the sink. A cold front drifted down her spine.

Without a word she fetched the dryer and got the hell out.

***

Norman cruised along the final stretch of traffic-choked freeway before Vic's place. He didn't accelerate only to slam the brakes as so many LA drivers did. The ride was therefore a chill 25 MPH, which would normally send Vic to dozing, except that Norman turned up the music so he and Hanna could sing along to a nursery rhyme at the top of their lungs.

"To market, to market, to buy a big fat pig, home again, home again, jiggity-jiggity-jig. To market, to market, to buy a big fat hog, home again, home again, jiggity-jiggity jog . . . "

A hundred choruses later, Norman glided the Subaru to the curb in front of La Villa Armada. "Home again, home again, little buddy."

Vic didn't want to be alone in his apartment. "Come up?"

Norman tapped the brim of his Dodgers cap. "Game starts soon."

Vic didn't move.

"I'll check on you in a few days," Norman pressed a button and Vic's seat belt whipped off. "The sisters have your key and Number One."

Vic nodded, twisted around to Hanna. "Bye, banana."

"Bye, dummy."

"I don't want to frighten you, kid, but I think my hand is up there waiting to kill me."

"Aw come on," Norman said.

"Sorry."

"Deepak says: 'Replace fear-based thinking with love-based thinking.' The click of the doors unlocking was Vic's cue to scram.

"Vic says f-u-c-k o-f-f."

Norman shook his head, turned up the nursery rhyme. He and Hanna sang again as Vic got out.

The front gate opened with ease—the sisters were efficient . . . and not sunning by the pool. Odd, especially since it was at least 90 degrees.

The stairs took forever. Each step hurt, for real and in his heart, heavy-laden as he was with images of what might be awaiting him . . . a ruined rug, broken furniture, a dog with PTSD, a marshal waiting to arrest him for attempted assault, a robot hand lying in wait, planning to sever him like it did to the thumb. Poor bastard never stood a chance.

Not only was he *not* killing it, he was sinking fast into the negative percentiles. The upside was a spanking new idea for a *Killing It* marketing tagline: "Kill it Before it Kills You."

Number One's happy yipping echoed around the courtyard as he scampered to Vic. The sisters trailed behind him, phony smiles plastered on their faces.

"Welcome back," said Cozy. Mamie handed him the key.

The sisters' attention shifted from hand bandaging to the staples and eyepatch, their eyes curious but empathetic. Vic gave Number One a bunch of kisses and then let him go in first. The sisters followed them inside but kept near the front door.

"Cozy did a fabo job on the rug," Mamie said. Vic nodded and tried on a smile. He had to agree it looked fine, except for the slight discoloration running from trunk to bedroom. So, except for that, yeah. Plus, the trunk looked better than ever.

"We're going to get a steam cleaner in here next week. I'll give you plenty of notice," Mammie said.

Cozy pointed to the stack of mail on his bistro table. "We put all your mail there."

"Thanks guys, I owe you one," said Vic. "Shit, I owe you a million."

Mamie threw Cozy a look then said, "We'll let you get to it, hon."

They hugged him goodbye, each casting a worried expression at the bedroom where Number One was engaged in a stare-down with the door.

***

Alone. Always alone. He'd die alone. The dog didn't count. He loved Number One, but someday he'd die and Vic would still be alone. No dog would change the fact that he was a loner. A man in exile. Shit. What if he *wasn't* alone? What if he was right and the thing was still here? Everyone thought he was nuts, but he'd seen that crawling motherfucker drag his poor thumb into the bedroom. It wasn't a hallucination from shock.

In an instant, Vic made a choice. Instead of dwelling on his fear, he'd flesh out the new marketing idea. People might call it avoidance; he preferred "entrepreneurial brainstorming."

"Kill it before it kills you." The more he thought about it, the more it became the perfect tagline for the app. Kill your bad diet. Your negativity. Your poor hygiene, and your bad habits, such as procrastination, which, according to Norman, had ruined Vic's life.

"Kill it before it kills you," he chanted, gathering enough momentum to move to the swords. Lefty grabbed the bladed sword, all clean and not a speck of gore. Vic scooted Number One away with his foot, entered the bedroom and closed the door behind him.

Nerves ululated in a pre-flight response; Lefty poised and ready to strike; Stumpy prepared to thwack any critter or sentient body part that dared move.

He visually divided the room into quadrants—bing, bang, boom, bam—the only anomaly being a postcard next to his phone on the bed. He had no memory of being on his phone in the bedroom or looking at a postcard. But there was a lot he didn't remember about the last few days.

***

From inside the closet, through a sliver of space where the door didn't connect to the wall, It watched the man's legs move about the room, kicking laundry, turning a circle until the knees faced the closet door. A blade hung down the side of the man's jeans.

When the closet slid open It made a hasty retreat into the darkness of an old duffel bag, where It could watch unseen. Only the man's eyes moved.

***

As with all procrastinators, Vic had the gift of self-bargaining and rationalization, convincing himself 100 percent killing it meant emptying the closet, which he wouldn't be doing today. Rolling the closet door shut, he assured himself 50 percent was good enough. He grabbed the phone and postcard and shut the door behind him on his way out. *Tomorrow, I do 65 percent,* he vowed.

Flipping over the postcard, he saw what he expected: LikeReal's foot-hand-eye logo. The edges of the images were furry thanks to shit Photoshop skills. "Fucking amateurs."

The postcard said, *Save the Dates. Which* meant a two-day visit to the lab . . . three days from now for the *final procedure*. Final procedure? Had they discussed a final procedure? Would it include final photos? *A little late now.*

He video conferenced Doctor Cord, not expecting an answer, since the last few attempts went unanswered.

Later, he slept on the couch and dreamed someone was weeping in his bedroom.

SHELLY LYONS

25.
PHANTASM 8

LOWER-LEVEL AIRSPACE ABOVE the Los Angeles basin was carefully segregated. Radar range began at 900 feet. Helicopters stayed upwards of 500 feet. News and paparazzi helicopters often took it down to 300, say if there was a horrible tragedy, or naked celebrity lovers in a backyard pool. Shopping drones were restricted to an altitude between 120-200 feet, that is, until they came in for delivery.

From the expanse of train yards and warehouses east of Chinatown rose the augmented Phantasm 8, an egg-shaped drone the size of a Brazil nut, glowing amber and humming like a power line as it pivoted into a north-by-northwest direction. Tonight its airspace would vary between 350 and 1800 feet, allowing for mountains.

Mission start time was 6:55 pm, the beginning of civil twilight, a 55-minute window in which the darkening sky and slight delay in automatic streetlights allowed the best chance of traveling unnoticed.

By 6:57 pm, the Phantasm 8 had accelerated to 65 MPH, navigating around power lines as it crossed the 110-downtown freeway, then skimmed the Griffith Park hills, and traveled alongside the north-bound 5 freeway above the LA river, snaking through Elysian Valley, Atwater Village, Glendale . . . past a news 'copter tracking the glut of cars . . . threading through a spate of ten-story buildings, over swatches of flat-box neighborhoods. It shot up to the max altitude as it crossed a section of the mighty Verdugo Mountains, then descended into the Sunland-Tujunga valley, a wind tunnel due to the surrounding mountains.

At 200 feet altitude, it weaved around busy shopping drones, then dipped below the tree line, where it slowed to 12 MPH.

If programmed, it could have easily recorded the sounds of television and conversations in the passing houses below, but that was not its directive.

Its Collision Avoidance Center didn't detect the swooping owl until it was too late, and the drone got caught in a clawed foot. The Phantasm 8 logged the species as the Western Screech Owl—pale grey; silent in flight—and electrified itself. Voltage crackled up the talons and the owl issued a high-pitched KRICK as it disengaged, flying off to easier prey.

Onwards, the object flew until it sailed over the gates of La Villa Armada, then idled in the courtyard, accessing: *Victor Moss, apartment 14*. It zipped over the roof to Vic's bedroom window. The volume of its humming grew significantly as it announced itself to someone inside.

Number One, home alone, barked at the sound until it stopped.

Several minutes later, the bedroom door opened.

26.

HENRY HATCH

THE NAME *Henry Hatch* was written on a note wrapped around her phone. That was it, a guy's name. No context. *Eddie got the better deal,* Tanya thought, handing the Tupperware filled with snickerdoodles to the hospital's Lost & Found person to give to him.

***

"These are all men," Crystal told Tanya as they crouched behind a bush at the edge of the community center lawn.

"It's a sausage party for sure," Tanya agreed.

Both women were dressed head-to-toe in black, with knit caps and black sneakers. Earlier, they'd taken selfies to document their spy apparel for posterity. Both were sad to note the more "drunk moms on Neighborhood Watch foot patrol" parallels rather than "asskicking lady spies."

Crystal was an actual drunk mom after the three-margaritas dinner preceding their mission, which had sounded so fun to Crystal when the idea was first pitched to her.

Tanya's googling had netted a single mention of Henry "Hank" Hatch in a community bulletin. Apparently, Hank was the featured speaker every other Wednesday night at a meeting called "You Can Overcome." *But overcome what?*

From their vantage point behind the huge shrub, the

women scoured tonight's arrivals—a parade of sadness for sure, but Tanya was hard-pressed to identify their collective issue.

"Maybe they'll gut a cat and drink its blood," Crystal suggested in a loud, slurry voice.

Tanya shushed her. Crystal shushed back.

"I'm going in," Tanya said.

"Noooo. It's too dangerous," Crystal got out before a huge belly laugh. "I'm sorry, I think that's the first time I've ever said those words. Oh, you know what sounds good right now? A hotdog."

"You can come with me, or you can stand here alone."

The women stared each other down. "This sucks," Crystal said. "Where's the ladies? All the ladies? There's no ladies!"

"Stay or come." Tanya pulled her cap further down over her hair, then crossed onto the lawn and headed towards the building. Crystal huffed, then weaved along after her.

***

The women chose seats closest to the exit and hunched down to blend in. Crystal whispered in Tanya's ear: "Do you ever find yourself the only woman in a group of men and even though you don't want to, you find yourself picturing how a gang rape might look?"

"Well, now I will, thanks!"

Crystal craned her neck around. "We could beat the hell outta any one of them. Except that guy maybe. He'd be work." Crystal nodded to Hank, who'd entered from somewhere in the back to hearty applause. He waved everyone quiet as he took his place behind the podium.

Neither woman knew this, but Hank now had a working eye, normal as the next guy's. He'd also transformed from frail to tight, like he'd been living in the gym. His LikeReal.net t-shirt strained against blossoming pecs and biceps.

Tanya scrawled *likereal.net* in her little notebook.

"Many of you have heard the story about how I lost my eye," Hank began. "Now I want to tell you how I grew a new one, and in the process learned to shed my fears and anger and regrets and be born anew. Not through our Lord, God bless him, but I've been there, done that, and will continue to do that. It's time to give birth to a version of myself who trusts in the Lord and *also* in my own powers."

The blind man sitting nearest to Tanya hollered an "Amen!"

"Amen, indeed," Hank said. "We are given life. Why should we expect divine protection? Shouldn't we work as hard to save our souls as He does? Why should we be immune from loss? We shouldn't! Because every loss teaches a lesson about how not to lose again."

Hank let it sink in. Lots of male voices murmured in the dark.

"I'm sure you've all noticed my shirt."

The blind man uttered, "I can't see shit."

***

Vic spotted Tanya the moment she stepped out from behind the large shrub—dressed like a cat burglar—and flitted across the lawn. Another woman trailed behind her. And every single dude noticed, but none would be caught looking. Tanya being here meant she was piecing together a larger story rather than a just-Vic piece. It rankled his pride a little bit.

He kept his distance from her. The eyepatch made him feel ugly and insecure, no matter how rad his hair looked. He snuck around to the back of the room and took a seat behind a tall man. Damn, Hank was a different guy. Bigger, sighted. *How did he fix his problem? Did he get another proto eye?*

Vic wanted to ask why Cord was ghosting him, and why Stephan acted like he was in charge. Also, what the hell about Hank's new eye? How did that happen? But he knew Tanya would probably stick around to talk to Hank as well, so he tiptoed out the door before the lecture ended.

Vic got in his car, dreading another night on the couch imagining sounds in the bedroom. Although Number One's vigilant growling and scratching on the bedroom door suggested these weren't imaginary. Something was in there, and Vic, too afraid to investigate, continued to give himself a pass on *Killing It*. Each day he expected less of himself.

As he drove to Doctor Cord's, Vic was struck by a brilliant idea. He'd create a pop-up window for when a guy reduced goal percentages more than say four days in a row and needed to get back on track. Vic pictured a square-jawed drill sergeant and maybe a word bubble that said *I Still Believe in Heroes!*

***

Before Vic was even halfway out of his car, Stephan's voice rang loud. "RSVP is in three days, Victor Moss."

Vic nonetheless marched forth, pressing the intercom button. "How come Hank has a new working eye and I have one damned hand?" He repeated the question more than a dozen times. The last three lost their oomph, and he was about to give up when the doors whooshed open. The sight of Stephan in a kimono robe was startling, as was the new addition to the lobby: a full suit of armor upright on a stand. If Vic wasn't so pissed off, he'd be all kinds of impressed by its mightiness.

Stephan trained his amber eyes on Vic's person, from head to toe. "It's not time yet, Victor."

"Time for what? Why can't I speak to the doctor?" Vic tried to step inside. Stephan blocked him. "How come Hank has an eye?"

"The doctor is indisposed."

"Maybe he won't be indisposed to a lawsuit for a malfunctioning prosthetic hand that sent me into the hospital, Stephan."

If he were capable of emotion, Stephan looked momentarily befuddled and let his guard down, allowing Vic a glimpse at the computations running behind those eyes. He was probably referencing hospital records.

"It is after-hours. Go home." Stephan stepped back inside. The doors closed.

"Motherfucker!" Vic pummeled the door with Lefty until it hurt. Kicked in the dick again. This time by an AI.

***

One thing most people didn't know about Tanya was that she's missing the end of her left pinkie finger. The old digitus manus minimus was two-thirds the other pinkie's size since birth. As a teenager, she took to wearing prosthetic tips, more as a fashion statement than an attempt at obfuscation, and every phase she went through saw an addition to her collection, from meticulously glued acrylic gems to the steampunk bronze with a tiny watch face on the tip. These days she went unadorned and kept her nail polish light.

Hank spotted the defect the moment she brought an oatmeal cookie up her to her lips. His eyes locked on so blatantly, it made Tanya's cheeks burn with a self-consciousness she'd not felt since sixth grade when the popular girls called her "Pinkie Lasagna."

In turn, she observed the bling on his t-shirt. Small but noticeable, the tiny button he wore featured a photo realistic drawing of a disembodied foot floating against a blue background. When she asked him about it, he ducked the question, instead telling her how lucky she was in attending tonight because it was his last. "Time for me to find other ways to help," he'd said, then suggested she, even with her "hardly noticeable abnormality," should check out LikeReal. His eyes flew back to the pinky.

***

"Bottom line," Tanya explained the following day to Cindy in the writer's bullpen, "all he would tell me was he got a new eye and it works perfectly, and then he hit on me in a really creepy way."

"Rutting piglets, all," Cindy spat, swinging her legs up onto her desk. "And you confirmed he was at the hospital because he tore out his own eye?"

"How does someone even do that?" Connor interjected as he plopped down on a bean bag chair. Yet another uninvited interruption that went unrebuked.

"You got a little chocolate milk moustache there, Conner," Tanya said.

"Ha, nice," Conner replied. "He's a baby, but he's growing . . . "

"I got confirmation from a hospital insider," Tanya told Cindy. "Apparently, the patient, Henry, repeatedly screamed about how the eye tore out on its own. I have the whole text from my source, but he's staying anonymous."

"Who is he?" Connor asked, tossing a Hacky Sack from hand to hand.

"His name is 'unnamed source.'" Tanya grunted herself off the bean bag. "Anyway, I'm going to check out the business tomorrow. It's near Chinatown."

"Ooh, while you're down there you should go to Yang Dragon," Cindy said.

"Fuck that, go to Alhambra if you want real Chinese food," Connor said.

"Yes," Cindy agreed, "but when in Rome."

Tanya had no intention of taking either of their recommendations. "I'll check in." Then, after a look at alpha-boy, fake-Aunty, and a white board filled with the same psycho shit she wrote in her notebooks—*incest cult . . . gangrene penis . . . monster truck vs tractor*—she decided this would be her last article for these dopes. She was perfectly capable of investigating the world's abnormalities without having to interact with tedious hipsters.

27.
SERGEANT JOAN

THREE MILES EAST as the crow flies, the bells of the Sacred Hearts parish tolled, their doleful sounds subdued by the expanse of freeways. Two miles west, the more strident clangs from the Cathedral of Our Lady of the Angels got half-drowned by wind updraft over the river. By the time Vic's ears received their stereophonic discord, the pealing was more insinuation than actual heralding of the midnight hour. The insinuation was doom. The kind of shit they play in Spanish horror movies while an old lady pushes her flower cart over cobblestones.

Vic listened to the dueling bells' conclusion from the confines of his Honda, which he'd parked by the abandoned warehouse next to Cord's place. From this vantage point, he'd still have a view of Cord's while staying outside camera range. Upon scouting for closer cameras around him, he'd seen a single broken remnant from the previous century and knew it wouldn't have eyes on him. He opened a turkey jerky stick for Number One, who he'd fetched from home, and poured some water in a bowl on the passenger side floor. He popped half an Ambien and reclined his seat.

***

The big rig thundered down the alley at 6 am, waking both Vic and the homeless guy sleeping on the hood of his car.

139

Vic checked Number One, still sound asleep in the passenger seat, then rolled down his window and negotiated a retreat for a 20-dollar bill, which the guy regarded from under the hood of a dirty coat.

Ahh! Vic remembered what he had in his trunk and ran to it, rifling around until he pulled out the one-man tent from that trip to Burning Man with Norman. The guy accepted the gift with a nod, and a probing stare at Vic's bandaging, before turning in the opposite direction and trudging down the alleyway. Vic later recalled never actually seeing the guy's eyes.

**

At a safe distance, the man dropped the tent and turned in Vic's direction, about 50 yards off. His amber eyes clicked, much like Stephan's, as he zoomed in for a close-up. The subject was still in the car, head back, eyes closed. He caught movement in the frame and panned to the little dog who spotted him, ears alert. The guy notched up his sound levels, and could hear the growling, too. Some darting creatures were better than others. Less acute. He clicked his jaw and spoke: "Victor Moss is parked outside." He then transferred the picture he took of Vic sleeping.

Stephan's voice responded, "We have a preemie situation. Subject is harmless but stay close."

**

This time Number One's vehement barking woke Vic. In his rearview mirror he saw an SUV pull into the lot, and park in the space closest to Cord's front door. Vic shook off the Ambien, but his vision wasn't acclimating quickly enough in the bright morning sun, so he didn't get a good look at the woman exiting the vehicle. He put on his sunglasses, but she moved quickly to the doors, and they swallowed her inside.

He hauled Honda ass towards Cord's, pulling up next to the SUV.

Two children clambered around in the back seat. Old enough to be out of baby seats, too young to be left alone with the windows up. A girl and a boy, maybe twins. He checked his phone for the temperature. 76 degrees at 10:01 am. Hmmm. They'd be okay for a while—but wait!—

Trash robot time!

He backed up the car so he and Number One could see past the SUV's butt. The show had already started. Trash Robot elongated its body, dumping a load into the bin as Number One danced from side to side, paws scraping along the base of the window. The bot crossed the alley and disappeared into its doggy door. Vic wondered what Number One would do if let loose. Chase it inside?

The children banged on their windows with tiny fists, shouting at him, but Vic couldn't hear a word. Something about their faces, though. They weren't smiling, which is what people usually did when they encountered Number One, his plucky ugliness being universally appealing. No, their faces wore expressions a bit more anxious. Pleading? Terrified?

Enough mystery. Vic got out to check on them. All the doors were locked. The kids pantomimed that they couldn't unlock from the inside. Momma must be using a new vehicle app to protect the kiddos from marauders and also to keep them from wandering off while she ran an errand, say, to visit the mad scientist.

Vic gave the kids a "what can I do" shrug but leaned against the SUV as if that'd comfort them. By this time, Number One was barking nonstop through his four inches of open window.

Behind him, little fists slapped the window hard enough that Vic turned, mouthing a 'sorry' and miming having no keys. The little boy's pleading look made it all the more difficult to shrug off. Those eyes, so deeply panicked, looked familiar. Oh shit, this was the kid from one of the LikeReal "After" photos.

Just then, the front door spit out Sergeant Joan. Vic rushed to meet her. She jumped at his sudden presence, then laughed at her reaction. "I didn't see you there, brother." She beeped her vehicle open, but the kids quickly slammed each lock down. "Well, the children are rejecting me. Same with the husband."

Vic noticed she wore a button with the image of the floating foot. She noticed he did not and backed away.

"Oh! I can't talk to you!"

"Wait! Why?" Vic pursued. "How come Cord let you in, but he's ghosting me?"

She continued beeping the doors open, but the kiddos were fast, hopping around the car and slamming them locked as fast as Joan could unlock them.

"Let me in!" She knocked on the windows.

"Please, can you tell me what's going on? Did you have troubles, too?" Vic persisted, but she wouldn't look his way.

Sergeant Joan finally faked out the little girl, threw open the driver's door and slid inside. The SUV screeched out of the lot in reverse. As the Sarge whipped it down the alley, Vic's last glimpse of the little boy was his faced pressed to the window. Vic waved, feeling like an asshole.

"Two days, Victor," Stephan's voice boomed from the loudspeaker. "Please return in two days."

Vic wanted to cry. Wanted to drive his car through those fucking doors, running straight over Stephan and his stupid turtleneck sweater. But, as per usual, he chose retreat, and chose to lie on the app by giving himself an A-minus for effort when it should have been a D-plus.

28.
THAT'S NOT MINE!

VIC AND NUMBER ONE spent the remainder of the day sitting poolside. Every neighbor dropped by. Ensconced in a deck chair underneath a big umbrella, Vic knew he was the "Special Guest," the "Scuttlebutt du jour," the "Mafia Don," "Patch." Neighbors had heard rumors, but nobody said the words "suicide" or "psychotic break" when, in ones or twos, they paid their respects. Main topics included September weather . . . "95 degrees on a fall day!" . . . and how everyone was ready for sweater weather. But their true hunger was for Vic's Big Story.

Vic complied, dispensing small bytes of info without the sci-fi elements. Each version was a variation of what he told the first neighbor who approached: "I had a situation with a malfunctioning prosthesis, and my eyelid was damaged in the process."

In between callers, Vic scoured Tanya's social media for any mention of the—what was it? Misunderstanding? Date gone awry? Perverted act? With a single post, she could destroy him. He'd be tried and hanged online, with strangers rendering judgment, advising Tanya to press charges, and immediate exile from the zeitgeist. His reputation murdered, career prospects dicey. And *Killing It* would never sell with his name attached. Tanya could do that so easily if she chose. He hoped for mercy.

When the swim instructor showed up, everyone watched Cozy paddle from shallow end to deep end to shallow end, wearing only padded armbands to keep herself afloat. She finished to applause. Vic reminded himself to add "good neighbors" to "Positive Thoughts."

Jun-ho and Yeong-jin fired up the grill for burgers, hotdogs, and corn on the cob. A neighbor delivered a plate containing all three to Vic, and an extra hot dog for Number One.

When the last neighbor was fed selective Vic deets, a consensus theory emerged: he cracked after a woman dumped him, and in a bid for her attention, he'd Van Gogh'd his prosthetic hand, tried to tear out his eyeball, and would have bled to death, if not for Mamie and Cozy.

Vic knew none of this. In his mind, he was Mysterioso, the hot, troubled neighbor with the eyepatch. Half his building was over 55, but what the hell. Let old ladies dream.

As night fell and the grill cooled, Vic took Number One out to do his business, and returned to an empty courtyard. The sisters and their fellas were gone. The neighbors were gone. Citronella candles, extinguished.

It was time to go upstairs.

***

He stood inside his door. Number One strained forward on the leash, but Vic held him firm. Everyone had been telling Vic, subtly or overtly, "it was all in his head," and if true, how come that fucking record was playing?

A live studio audience applauded. "Thank you, thank you very much," said Bob Newhart. "Uh, many of you may have read *The Hidden Persuaders*. It's about advertising. And one of the points the book made is that the real danger of the public relations man or the advertising man was that they were creating images—"

Vic yanked out the stereo's plug, removed his bladed katana from its mount, and dragged Number One back to the pool patio where man and dog slept on a deck chair.

Sometime during the night, a neighbor covered them with beach towels.

***

The rooster crowed. Vic opened his eyes to a dark courtyard. Dawn was on its way. Number One peed on a mini palm tree. Vic wished he could simply lift his own leg on a plant or squat on the grass, but his business had to be conducted upstairs.

The first goal for the day popped into his head: stop speculating a worst-case scenario. Why do this to himself? Maybe his stereo was haunted. Or he'd been losing track of how long to wait between Percocets or Ambien—Goal 2: tapering off—and maybe he himself had put on Newhart as a way of channeling good memories of Paps. With that explanation and his daily goals in place, Vic, Number One, and the blade returned home.

Inside, the stereo remained silent. Still, he kept the sword with him as he slogged to the bathroom. The toilet's lid was shut. Odd. Using the sword's tip, he raised the seat and lid together, choking a scream at the porous spool of ombre-hued ghastliness within.

"THAT'S NOT MINE!"

Vic barged into the living room, every hair on his body rising for the occasion. The dog wasn't there. Neither was one of the wooden swords—the bigger, heavier one. THUMP! Pain splintered across his skull. Stars burst in his eyes. He dropped to his knees.

Number One, cowering under the bistro table, barked incessantly.

The wood katana swung diagonally for what would surely be a killing blow, had Vic not swung the sword blade back over his head. KATHUNK!

Wood and steel met in a real *Highlander* moment. Steel won, eating half the wood in a single clash. Vic hitched the blade forward—wood sword still attached— bringing a new-fangled weapon to bear: a steel and wood cross.

Vic sprung to his feet, dizzy and nauseated. He stumbled over a pair of slippers so unthinkingly discarded in the middle of the floor and crashed headfirst into the Hoo Maru painting, spraying blood on its sails. He'd also dropped the joined weapons.

The looming shadow pounced, grabbed him by the neck. A thumb pressed on his carotid. Vic couldn't breathe, flailing, raking the assailant's arm with Lefty and impotently punching with his stump.

Though his blood-soaked vision was for shit, he saw his attacker's face: an exact replica of himself, if a bit dewy around the edges, with two eyelids and no goddamned scar. Its eyes smoldered with fear and adrenaline. Its mouth made weird choking noises, but then so did Vic's.

Lefty clawed for the sword handle, but the pinkish blood under its nails was slippery, so his fingers made no purchase. He wiped Lefty on the carpet, managed a solid grip, and swiped up.

The—thing—clone—*New-Vic* ducked, releasing its death clutch. The blade missed by a hair, but the wood walloped New-Vic's cheek like a pimp with a cudgel, and a dawn of hot pain rose swiftly through new nerve-endings, burning his ability to move or think. he could do was hold its jaw and blubber.

Getting a wee break as the clone floundered, Vic scrambled to his feet, grabbed the blade's handle and stomped on the bokuto to extricate it from the bladed katana—Vic-tory! He whipped it at New-Vic, blade arcing down.

New-Vic sidestepped its sweep, somersaulted over to grab the wood katana, and landed in fight stance like a fuckin blade master.

"Goddammit!" Vic's blade got stuck in the rug and padding beneath. Vic almost pissed himself in panic, yanking frantically as the baying clone came for him, bokuto en route to Vic's skull. "Motherfucker!" Vic tore up a swath of carpet, the blade emerged, and he twisted for a strike—too late—THWACK!—the wood landed square in Vic's chest. A rib cracked. Vic's feet gave out. He gulped for breath from a prone position on the floor.

New-Vic took his sweet time exchanging wood for blade, then strolled over to his progenitor, who flopped around like a trout. He paused as his brain received a quick info byte about a fishing trip with Dad when Vic was forced to bang a fishy dead with a pipe so fishy would suffer no more. *Death is mercy*, thought New-Vic, raising his sword. "This sword will deliver you, and free me," he said in a near-perfect approximation of Vic's voice.

Vic threw a Hail Mary: "Hey, what's that thing behind you?" The clone's eyes widened, and he spun around in fight stance—giving Vic time to roll out of his line of attack and around to the front of the couch, where he jumped to his feet. The clone seemed shocked by the ground movement but recovered and vaulted over the couch in pursuit.

Vic used Stump and Lefty to lift the trunk for a block. The sword grazed the trunk and slipped from the clone's hand. A frustrated grunt. Vic heaved the trunk, pressing it against the monster, squashing him onto the couch as the thing flailed beneath.

Vic's eyes darted, spotted the closest sword—one of the bokutos. A last shove on the trunk until he heard a slight crack, then Vic ran for it.

Behind him the trunk flew airborne and New-Vic sprang up, just in time to see wood freighting through the air. The katana cuffed his head with a horrible thud, and New-Vic belly-flopped onto the couch.

Vic waited. The thing didn't move. Vic wiped Lefty's sweat and blood on his jeans. Checked to see if Number One was okay. Poor fellow had pissed the carpet in the dining nook.

New-Vic's head rose, pink ribbons mucking his face. He tried to crawl, got a leg off the couch. Drool spilled from his mouth. He spat out blood and a molar, looking surprised by that. Vic awaited his eventual collapse, but New-Vic had other ideas, springing off the couch with a speed heretofore unknown to Vic, who could only make an O face as he was tackled and shoved backward like a football sled. His head slammed into the Hoo Maru, and the wall knocked him senseless.

***

A woman's foot rested on a pillow. Vic's lips—were they Vic's?—descended from above, a Deus ex machina blowing hot puffs of air on each red-polished toe, and each toe curled with pleasure. He trailed up the arch to the tune of a woman's soft moaning. Traveling north to the shins, blowing, blowing. A playful nibble on the calf. A woman's slight gasp followed by a giggle. Languorously journeying up her leg, thigh hairs pricked in the wake of his breeze. Over the pelvis—ignoring the hairy blossom for now—and up to hips bucking and churning for release. Up, up, he blew, over the breast and adamant nipple, to the armpit and Tanya's Technicolor hibiscus tattoo. His lips mashed upon its petals, kissing each and every one; flowers throbbed as he traced each letter of "Namaste" with his tongue. The lips drew back, exposing razor-sharp teeth that sank into the tattoo, tearing up the petals, consuming letters, the gorging of a starving beast. The woman's shriek cut short—

***

Vic and his clone woke up at the exact same moment. Vic was slumped against the wall in his living room, where blood dripped down the Hoo Maru's sails into the ocean.

New-Vic sat behind the wheel of the Honda, which was parked across the street from Tanya's yoga studio. Both faces were blighted by lacerations and bruises. Each discovered clumps of blood on his hairline. Each blotted it with their stump—Vic's right, New-Vic's left.

29.
DIVERGENCE

THE CRACKED RIB discharged bullets of pain into his lungs as Vic surveyed the aftermath of battle through one fuzzy eye . . . a fucked-up painting, a cracked trunk, carpet torn up. Blood. Cozy and Mamie would be thrilled. No dog. "Number One? Buddy?"

***

Dawn peeked over the mountains. New-Vic glanced at the ugly dog curled on the passenger seat. Despite the wiry hair and a musty smell he couldn't identify, he stroked the dog's head and was pleased when it pushed into the touch as if enjoying it. No trace of suspicion in its doleful eyes, so different from the kicking and screaming mutt he extracted from the apartment on his way out. It took some muscle and a handful of dog biscuits before the dog calmed down. Truth be told, the biscuits weren't bad. Crunchy. Chicken flavored. And boy did he love chicken. *I love chicken?* he thought, uneasy, still dealing with bursts of information from his second-hand brain fibers. His eyes felt heavy. *Rest is required*, he thought, letting sleep take him.

***

The real Vic Moss popped a Tylenol with an orange juice chaser, then roamed his apartment, calling for Number One in an increasingly pitiful voice. He opened the bedroom door and entered clone HQ. Something had definitely slept in his bed, leaving behind a helix of blankets and sheets as though sleep had been fitful. The downy feather pillow retained a head indentation. A glimpse under the bed explained why he was running low on cereal bowls and spoons. He counted four bowls under there. But no dead dog, a tremendous relief.

In his closet, all of his casual work jackets hung in a row, followed by tees and hanging pants cubbies. Nothing changed. But there was something inside his old golf shoes. Vic leaned closer. *Jeez!* A pile of Popeyes chicken bones. Vic got Popeyes at least twice a week. But in his haze of recovery, he perhaps didn't keep track of how many pieces he ate. Or didn't eat. Or did the thing vulture through his garbage at night? The police must have seen this and chalked it up to Vic's general weirdness.

He went back out to the living room to confirm that the key hook by the front door was empty, as was the leash hook. Number One was alive, at least.

***

New-Vic woke with a start a few hours later, confused that the darkness was gone, yet the murky gray car windows obstructed his view of the yoga studio. He sifted through circuitry, seeking any image or memory of gray car windows. There was a time when the progenitor was kissing a female in the car. Beyond the windshield, the beams of two headlights disappeared on an expanse of empty beach. The longer they kissed, the heavier their panting, the dimmer the beach got. Ah! Moisture condenses on the inside of windows if the outside air is cooler than inside. Heat from kissing or from breathing created the fog. Deduction!

He got out and crossed the street to the studio, tried the door but it would not open. A peek in the window showed him the place was empty. Also empty was the decorative box hanging to the side of the door. *That's where the schedules go*, he thought, heading back to the car. Aside from this blip of not finding Tanya, the day was a success so far, what with the fog deduction and the driving. Seemed his Vic circuits, his Vic-cuits, as the progenitor would say, were firing at one hundred percent.

***

Instead of going to the hospital for aching ribs, Vic began wrapping his chest in duct tape—an ambitious feat when done single-handedly. What helped was repeating a William Riker quote like a mantra. "You do an end run around me again, I'll snap you back so hard you'll think you're a first-year cadet again."

***

For a baby driver, New-Vic handled the car proficiently, but wasn't clear on where he was heading. He searched his brain for the address of Vic's work, but the moron retained so little. The Honda was cruising through a sunny green suburb when it finally came to him. He had to make a left to get to the freeway. "Left turns, left turns . . . " The dog's ear twitched at the sound of his voice. "We hate left turns . . . I hate left turns." He had a second thought. "Not *hate*. I guess I just don't like them." He flicked the indicator with his left stub.

As timing would have it, at about 500 feet out, an old man with a cane and a cup of 7-Eleven coffee pressed the walk button, waited for the in-pavement crosswalk lights to blink, then took a few spry steps before noticing the Honda wasn't slowing down.

Discombobulated by the lights, New-Vic had forgotten to take his foot off the gas.

The Old man froze. *If this is it, make it quick and final*, he prayed.

New-Vic snapped to, stomping the brake. Number One flew against the glove box and dropped to the floor. New-Vic's neck whipped back and forth. "Oh no," he said, feeling a different type of adrenaline than what he experienced that morning. More terror. Less rage. A dollop of pity.

The old man gestured with his coffee for New-Vic to drive past.

The car window glided down. New-Vic waved him

forward with his left stump, which looked a tinch bigger than it had a few minutes ago.

"Proceed!" New-Vic hollered. But the old man shook his head "no" and emphatically urged him forth. New-Vic shrugged but took a bit too long pressing the gas pedal, which the old man interpreted as stubborn refusal, so resumed his trek. New-Vic shot forward, then slammed the Honda to a stop, inches from the terry cloth of the old man's walking pants. New-Vic banged on the horn, which caused the old man to spill some of his coffee.

"Oh no!" New-Vic cried.

After a glare that could set a kid's toy on fire, the old man hurled the coffee at the car.

A spray of Hazelnut coffee stung the laceration on his hairline. New-Vic steered the Honda around him, wondering why he'd been polite to such a mean old rotting thing.

***

Limping into the carport, torso wrapped in duct tape, Vic confirmed his parking space was empty, and quailed to a squatting position, hugging his knees and weeping helplessly. His ribs sent an S-O-S to his brain despite the "bandaging," but what the fuck did he care? He'd been trapped in what once was a baby spider web, but now found himself in a kill cocoon with nil hope of escape. And that thing was driving his car, with his dog, and his total personage, minus the ugly scar and missing eyelid, which was so goddamned unfair. He reached for any words or thoughts to comfort himself. There was the drunk-driving incident in Tijuana in high school. He got past that, didn't he? Or the trip in the convoy where he struggled to reconnect to the satellite feed, while sounds of explosions shockwaved the van. He thought he'd detonate in a Massive Ordnance Air Blast. But he didn't, did he?

Vic unfurled. How did it know how to drive? Was it a Neo scenario? Did it run a program, say, "I know driving?" then steal his fucking car keys?

And where the hell was it going?

As he trudged upstairs to put on more clothes, his thoughts remained pragmatic—about the business of getting to work and the lie he'd tell Norman when he got there. He skirted past the big picture, not worrying about prostheses coming alive and transforming into homicidal doubles, focusing instead on how and where a guy might dispose of a clone carcass.

Two more Tylenols and the last half of a hospital pill hardly quelled the rib pain as he pulled on clothing items. The second eyepatch in his two-pack was missing, but he ignored the alarming implication of that. Locating his phone between couch cushions, he crowed, "Ha! You missed something!" Alas, the power bars were empty, and no charger to be found. Vic remembered he left it in the car.

One Harry Styles t-shirt, casual gray jacket, and skinny jeans later, he was knocking on the sisters' door. All the fighting and yelling in his apartment this morning, and nobody had stirred. Was he the neighbor who went crackers so often that everyone was inoculated to it?

Mamie opened the door, her sleep mask at half-mast. "Oh gee, what's wrong now, hon?"

"My car is missing—"

"Someone stole your car? Did you call the police?" She cinched the diaphanous robe around her teddy.

"No, borrowed. I'm handling it. But see, my phone is dead so I can't call a Lyft, so can drive me to work? I'll add 60 to the rent."

She waved it off. "Buy us donuts and we're good."

"Thanks, Mamie."

"I'm Cozy, hon."

"Oh sorry—"

"Kidding! I'm Mamie. Give us a minute."

She disappeared into the hallway where she knocked on a door and said, "Get dressed and get yer face on, hon! And find Jun's keys!"

Vic ventured no further than the doorway, admiring the luxurious modern decor in shades of pink and red, the four-foot-tall ceramic Venus statue, a rug fluffy as cotton candy.

Cozy plodded down the hallway, fully clothed and make-up free, which took ten years off her visage, with no paint or eyelash canopies to granny-fy her.

"Morning, hon," she said before digging into a blown glass bowl containing keys and coins. "Mars is in retrograde, so we're all effed up in our own ways right now, aren't we?"

Vic nodded.

"I mean, I was doing good with the swimming yesterday, but I had a gnarly dream last night and now I'm freaked again." She fished out a large, shiny BMW key fob.

"You did great yesterday, and you can only get better," said Vic.

She smiled, a tad flirtatiously, as was her way. "Lemme go get fixed." She pirouetted to the hallway where Jun-ho stood, wearing a frilly pink robe.

"What's going on?" Jun-ho asked her in Korean.

Cozy told him in Korean to "Go get dressed."

Jun-ho wavered, face suspicious.

"Gagi! Gagi!" she ordered, herding him down the hall.

***

Jun-ho's BMW, with its beige leather coolness and digitally blinged-out console panel, was the absolute most bitchin' thing Vic ever rode in, and if he were lucky enough to one day own such a car, he'd name it Ace Face.

Despite his awe and wonderment, Vic looked and felt like a discarded husk in the back seat. Mamie, seated next to him, cast a watchful eye as he dipped in and out of cat naps. Cozy sat co-pilot to Jun-ho, who pressed a button on his wheel, skidding the radio through stations until he landed on an oldies Korean station, catching 1990s K-Poppers Seo Taiji and the Boys rapping about love.

***

New-Vic's first encounter with a parking lot went great. He knew which building to park near and right-turned into a space marked JMS Consulting. Memories of actual work duties were vague but would clarify like everything else once he had to perform them.

Even in his haste to get the hell out of La Villa Armada, he'd taken a few minutes to ensure he'd pass physical inspection. Bruises were a problem he'd explain by citing a fall. The fake scar, made with a heap of beige acne cream mixed with a little ketchup, looked real enough, too. As a final touch, he stole one of Vic's eyepatches. According to his brain logs, it went over the left eye. He wore a t-shirt with Charles Bukowski's face on it under a blazer with elbow patches. The skinny jeans smelled clean, too. The slippers were a last-minute addition. He saw them, and even realizing that people wore shoes outside, it would take too long to remove the shoes the conked-out progenitor wore or find other shoes in the closet. Plus, slippers were quicker. As he slid them on, he thrilled at seeing his sprouting toenails.

Although First-Vic was missing his right hand, New-Vic's left hand looked odd. He had to chance it, so chose the left glove. As he slipped it on, he ruminated on his infancy spent in its interior, thrust into darkness and sensory deprivation where flexing and spasming did nothing but pinpoint the perimeters of his leather prison.

Now I wear my cage, and it doesn't wear me.

"I'll be back soon," he told Number One. He knew animals didn't speak or understand English. But this one seemed special.

Once inside the reception area, New-Vic accessed memories, smiled at the pretty receptionist, who wore a headset. "Good morning . . . " *bunhead, doer-but-she-cray-cray . . . Kendra . . . Key . . .* "Keisha."

Keisha, listening to someone on her headset, waved her nails at him. "No, you check his damn phone, and you stay strong!"

"I will," New-Vic replied, brain accessing an image of the ugly red-haired boss . . . Chet. Chet who owed him something, but no image surfaced, just the general impression of Chet as a bad guy. Vic theorized that the ugliness came not from genetics or lifestyle, but rather a misshapen soul always threatening to escape by oozing out his humongous pores.

Turn left. New-Vic turned left, clocking the sign that said "The Hive" with an arrow pointing in the same direction he was heading. *Go Vic-cuits!*

Sunil—*works the helpdesk, lives with three roommates*—was engrossed in laptop maintenance for a muscular middle-aged primate in tight pants. No name came to him except . . . *Frat Fuck?*

"Good morning, Sunil, good morning, Frat Fuck," New-Vic said, heading into The Hive. Frat Fuck snapped his gum.

Inside The Hive, Norman and Amy grunted good-mornings but didn't look up from their terminals as New-Vic took a seat at the empty desk in the corner. *This must be my desk, but it doesn't look . . . correct.*

As confirmation, Sunil popped his head in from the Help Desk room. "That is my work area, what do you need?"

New-Vic waved a sorry and moved over to the other empty desk. *His desk. My desk.*

***

Ace Face idled in the drive-thru donuts line, and Vic couldn't wait any longer—he had to contact Norman. "Can I get my cell?"

Cozy picked it up. "It's only at 6 percent, hon."

"That's fine."

She shrugged, unplugged it from the charge and handed it back to him. "Were you in a fight?"

"Yeah."

"Did you win?"

"No."

"Were you fighting with yourself again, hon?" Mamie asked as gently as she could.

"No."

Jun-ho passed a glazed twist to Vic. "They gave us a free one," he said in English.

The BMW pulled out into traffic. Vic wolfed the donut, licked his fingers, and texted Norman: *running L8. Car issue.*

"Hey." Mamie's voice.

Vic looked up from his phone, having just decided not to respond.

"Let's fix you up a little, hon," she reached for his face, beige goop on her fingers.

"What?"

"Let's cover those bruises just a tinch, hon. Cozy, do you have the under-eye stuff and some blush?"

"Of course."

"I'll be gentle, hon."

***

New-Vic had the LikeReal page open to the photo gallery, specifically to the photo of "Dean Winger." The progenitor had picked his own fake name, his dream name, and the one he'd give to ladies he met offline who he wanted to hook up with but never see again. Dean Winger was a motocross rider and international sales consultant. Also a creep.

Norman kept a covert eye on Vic, brow furrowing upon noticing Vic typing with his right hand. He recalled Vic's first big one-handed challenge—at least that Norman bore witness to—with the pickle jar, and how Vic had finally opened the lid by using his knees and his left hand. A BLOOP alerted him to a text. From Vic? *running L8. Car issue.* For cryin' out loud, what was this?

Dean Winger's "Before" image showed the progenitor with the scabby stump, and the "After" was the same photo but with a question mark covering the stump. Just then, Norman's message popped up on his screen with a BLOOP sound. *Did you just text me?*

New-Vic replied: ?

Norman removed his earbuds and spun to Vic. "Are you working on a new app?"

"I'm working. On work."

"Did you or did you not just now, 25 seconds ago, text me?"

New-Vic ignored his increased heart rate, kept his voice measured. "Oh, yeah, a robo app. I'll disable the timer, but you may get a few more before it takes." His time was running out in this place. Old-Vic was on his way.

Norman clucked appreciatively. "Apps for people trying to establish alibis. Very niche, very niche." He chuckled, re-inserting the earbuds.

New-Vic beamed at his approval. *I am happy when Norman is pleased with me,* he thought, then discarded the smile, perplexed by it all. As a newbie without the proper assimilation cast into a suspicious and easily panicked world, what was he to do? In lieu of an answer, his brain received multiple images of a flower painted on skin, and the shoulder and face and body to which it was attached. Tanya. He clicked to Google, typed: *kundalini burbank tanya* and found the yoga studio's site.

New-Vic pushed back from his desk, walked over to Norman. "I have a doctor's appointment."

"OK," Norman said, noting the Vic's hand stuck in his pants' pocket. He was certain Vic was lying but couldn't dispute the obvious medical needs.

"Namaste," New-Vic said, slippers chuffing across the carpet as he headed out the door.

***

On his jog back to the car, New-Vic spotted the swath of red 200 yards off. Chet on his Segway. He hopped into the Honda, revved its four-cylinders, and raced after the red-haired man, accessing pieces of a dream Vic had about riding a far-superior Segway in pursuit of . . . Chet was the name. When he'd caught up, he flung himself off his

Segway, tackled Chet, beat him to a pulp, pulling off chunks of ginger fur, and then his actual head.

New-Vic slowed the car, gliding alongside the ginger prick, reaching out the window with his stump, which had sprouted finger nubs, to point menacingly at Chet.

"You owe me something and you're going to give it to me Monday or you're in big trouble, bro-ho. Or else!" New-Vic gave him a trigger finger with his index and thumb nubs, then roared off, tearing through the lot at a whopping 15 MPH.

Chet watched him use an indicator to turn left into the main driveway, tapping the brakes like an old woman, and imagined the paper trail he'd need to cut that fruit-loop loose for good.

30.
STEPHAN CAN'T ANSWER THAT QUESTION

TANYA MADE A 9:30 am appointment with a voice on the phone belonging to someone named Stephan. This gave her 40 minutes before she had to teach Bliss class, AKA ladies of leisure weekday yoga.

She pressed the intercom button next to the large door adorned with the company's logo, which split into two as the doors opened to either side.

Her first view was a suit of armor, complete with battle-ax and helmet, an odd touch in the otherwise atomic-age bachelor pad aesthetic. She made a mental note to use the phrase "atomic-age bachelor pad" in her article. Then she noticed the mirror-paneled walls. Dozens and dozens of smaller and smaller Tanyas frowned at her. Every iteration could stand to lose ten pounds.

"Good morning, Teresa?" a friendly voice chirped from her left, where a handsome young android rose from behind his glass reception desk. Befitting the room's aesthetic, he wore groovy flared black pants, a mustard-colored sweater and a white cravat.

Unnerved by his realness, it took her a moment to remember she gave him a fake name. "Yes. I am Teresa. Hello."

"I am Stephan. Why don't you take a seat? Doctor Cord will soon be with you."

Tanya's heel caught on the rug, and she lurched forward, catching herself gracelessly, and then deciding to make a joke curtsy. *What am I doing?* she thought, helplessly committed to the bit. "Obviously, I have ballet training."

Stephan's laugh—"ho-ho-noo-hee-hee"—further unsettled her. *Did a programmer with a sense of humor think the laugh was cute?* Stranger than that, *why would they create a completely realistic human duplicate, but leave it with eyes the color of Halloween contact lenses?*

Another set of doors split open, and Doctor Cord entered, hand extended for a shake from the get-go. He wore similar pants to the android's, but with a white sweater and a yellow cravat. He and his robot coordinated wardrobe choices. *Adorbs.* He also wore the same button as Henry Hatch.

"Henry referred you to us, how wonderful," Doctor Cord said in a rich baritone. "He's one of my greatest achievements. The eyes . . . I assume you've seen the eyes?"

"Oh, right, yes, I couldn't tell which was real."

"They're both real . . . *like* real."

Was she expected to clap for him? Laugh?

"Was it a transplant?"

"He couldn't afford an eye transplant, and insurance felt that going through life with a single eye wasn't enfeebling enough to warrant coverage. This is where LikeReal came in."

"Right. So, Henry told me his first eye didn't 'take,'" she said, trying to keep it casual, chatty, the concerns of a future patient. "Has that happened to other patients? I mean, I'd need to know efficacy rates before I agreed, you know . . ."

The Doctor's tan whitened a little. "He told you his eye didn't take?"

"Yeah."

"When did he tell you that?"

"I'm not sure. When I met him, I guess . . . Wednesday."

The doctor and his android exchanged a look. Tanya knew she'd screwed up, but not how, though it had something to do with the timing.

"Or maybe it was two Wednesdays ago? I'm terrible with time," she said. The air in the room was as cold as the change in Doctor Cord's face.

"I'm sorry you had to travel all the way down here, but at this time we're not accepting new patients," Cord said. "However, I wanted you to meet me, so perhaps when we get an opening, we could let you know."

Tanya's cover was blown. But she needed a quote, at least. "Before I go, can you tell me, is prosthesis rejection a possibility? And have any others experienced malfunctions?"

Doctor Cord turned his back halfway through her ultra-reporter-like questions and vanished through his door before she finished her sentence.

"Sorry, did I say something . . . ?" She made a last stab. "Stephan, did the Doctor create you?"

"Yes." It sounded sarcastic. But it couldn't be sarcasm, not from a machine. Stephan pressed a button, re-opening the front door. He and his cravat subtly backed her towards it.

"Did the doctor also treat a man named Victor Moss? Or Dean Winger?"

"I can't answer that question," he said, "however, I thank you for coming. Please have an enjoyable day."

"Does the American Medical Association—" His long arm and beautiful hand gently pushed her past the threshold before the doors closed.

31.
MUTUALLY ASSURED
DESTRUCTION

ACE FACE THE BMW deposited Vic in front of the building. Cozy and Mamie waved goodbye as Vic headed inside, anxiety levels peaking.

In the lobby, hoping the makeup wasn't too obvious, he waved at Keisha, who was yacking on her headset. "Tell her you'll break off her trashy-ass acrylics if she puts another hand on him ... " She waved back. " ... You're too trusting." Vic paused at her desk. "Hold on, Mom." Keisha cupped the mouthpiece, raised her eyebrows at him.

"Have you seen me before now?" he asked.

"At least 800 times."

"No, today. Have you seen me today?"

"I'm looking at you."

"Did you see me come in to work today, previous to right now?"

"I don't keep track of employees, I'm not your damn time clock."

"Am I in there right now?"

"Go see for yourself." Vic nodded, rooted to the spot. "Go! Be industrious." She mad-dogged him until he exited, then un-cupped the microphone. "Remember, I told you about the one-handed yo-yo calls his hand 'Lefty?' Uh-huh ... 'Lefty can do it' ... 'Lefty's ramping up,' Lord ... "

To Vic's ear, The Hive's door creaked open like the

Haunted Mansion. Inside, the combination of brightness from the outside hallway and darkness inside created a dusk atmosphere. Good. Decreased the chances of scrutiny. His vision adjusted, and he was relieved to see his empty desk. Whew. *No clone fight at the office today.* He plopped into his chair. "Morning," he yelled over the 80s dance synth. Must been Amy's turn for "morning music choice."

Norman removed his earbuds. "Forget something?"

Vic's heart plummeted. So, it happened. Life-takeover, step one. "This is going to sound insane, but have I been here already? Today?"

Amy paused the music for some blatant eavesdropping.

"Yes . . . ?" To Norman the real question was: Is this guy all here right now?

"I sat at my desk?"

"You worked."

"Where am I right now?"

Norman's blood pressure burbled. *Is Little Buddy in the grips of a nervous breakdown?*

"You're sitting here talking to me, Vic."

"Yeah, I see you, too," Amy said.

"Not talking to you." Vic rolled his chair closer to Norman. "When did I leave?"

"Not more than five minutes ago." Norman noticed Vic was wearing a different t-shirt. Earlier, it was the old grizzled drunk man standing next to a hooker. Now it was the pretty man with bedroom eyes.

"Did I say where I was going?"

"Doctor's appointment."

"That's it? Nothing else?"

Norman rubbed the old brain cap, but nothing came.

Rolling back to his terminal, Vic wondered if the clone fellow was going to Cord's. *Is today the RSVP date?*

"You also said 'Namaste,'" Amy chimed in. "Thought I'd tell you even though you're not talking to me."

"Shit." Vic tapped his screen, saw the yoga schedule; cursor resting on Tanya's 10:30 class. Tanya!

Vic hunted-pecked furiously on his keyboard. *Can I pls borrow your car?*

BLOOP. Message received by Norman, who responded: *what happened to yours?*

BLOOP. If you want to come w me right now I tell u whole story.

BLOOP. I have a meeting.

BLOOP. I'm already on your insur as a 2nd driver. plz!

Amy's head oscillated between the men as they attacked their keyboards, sighing, reading, typing again. Neither uttered a word. Finally, Norman held out a car key, which Vic snatched after flashing a grateful smile at his pseudo dad.

"Get a room," she said, resuming the music.

Vic barreled down the hallway. Chet pointed at him from across a valley of cubicles, gesturing for him to come over. Vic gave him a helpless shrug as he veered into the reception area.

***

11:35 am. Kundalini students trickled out of class. From his vantage point across the street in the Honda in a red zone, New-Vic waited for a glimpse of Tanya. He'd spent hours letting her image permeate all his circuitry. Where was she? The dry winds stung his eyes, making the tears he knew of from Vic's memories. That pussy cried way too much, and dehydration was to be avoided.

***

Vic steered Norman's Subaru into a space in the middle of the block that allowed a good view of the yoga studio door. He noted the location of his Honda 100 feet behind him on the same side of the street. If the clone was here, it was waiting for Tanya, which meant she had yet to appear. And if that fucker did something untoward to her and further compounded Vic's past indiscretion, it wouldn't matter whether the thing lopped off his head; life would end either way. He checked the car clock: 11:39. Mr. Lake emerged, no doubt walking on sunshine with farts in his wake.

***

11:43. Still no Tanya. New-Vic jumped at Number One's sudden movement, paws on the dashboard, wet nose sniffing the air. *Why was the dog doing this?*

***

11:45. Tanya! New-Vic and Vic pepped up at her appearance. She wore a hoodie over her form-fitting yoga pants and a backpack with her mat sticking out the top.

New-Vic sank down in his seat so she didn't notice him. She disappeared around the edge of the building, and he popped up again. *Where did she go?!*

***

Vic saw Tanya enter the parking lot in his driver's side mirror. A moment passed, then a Vespa emerged and hung a left onto the street. Tanya! Adorable in a helmet decorated with hibiscus stickers.

He crouched down as his own car drove past, waited a beat, then started the Subaru. His ribs thrummed like angry little drums.

***

Inside Tanya's helmet, the tinkling sounds of a 60s pop chanteuse provided a perfect score for her ride home on this cooler, smog-free day. She hung a right, followed by a Honda and a Subaru.

A block down, a pregnant lady pushed a stroller across the street. A dog with dead back legs rolled alongside her in his titanium walking apparatus.

Tanya's Vespa stopped. Then the Honda. Then the Subaru.

The dominos fell fast. Tanya noticed New-Vic, who she thought was just plain old Vic wearing an eyepatch, as if following her from work wasn't eerie enough. New-Vic noticed her noticing him, then caught sight of the original Vic in his rearview mirror. Vic noticed Clone-Vic noticing him—thus ensued a confusing crisis punctuated by a trio of gasps, and Number One in the Honda's hatchback window, arfing at his real master.

***

"Oh, hell," Tanya muttered as she veered around the woman and her menagerie. The cars, less nimble, had to wait, affording Tanya a head start as she sped up to 45 MPH, drove up a driveway, along a sidewalk, and down to 30 MPH to round a sharp corner. She cut through an alley, emerging just as the Honda passed the street above. *God, did he see me?* She accelerated back up to 45, 50, careening around a corner and into the driveway of her duplex.

The Vespa barely stopped before she dismounted and bounded across the lawn, jostling her key fob as she ran to the door. She beeped it unlocked, zipped inside, hurdled over an ottoman covered in shoes, and shut her curtains. The room in darkness, she retreated into the kitchen, unsure of what to do next.

***

New-Vic spotted the toppled scooter half resting in a driveway, half on the lawn, but drove several more blocks at top speed, racing around corners until he was sure he'd lost the Subaru.

When the orb had visited him with instructions, New-Vic was disheartened to learn that while the actual birth cycle was complete assimilation of the host—allowing the carbon and the circuits to merge into something better—a perceived threat of destruction had disrupted his process, forcing baby New-Vic to detach prematurely, utilizing whatever torn-off carbon bits remained after the separation. The orb related a similar experience about an eye misinterpreting a migraine as certain death and therefore separating too soon.

In a normal gestation, the host was absorbed. No pain. No violence. However, in his abnormal situation, it was explained that he must eliminate the progenitor, or bring him to LikeReal and let them do it. In a normal gestation, he might not have had such crazy burning feelings for Tanya. Nor been possessed by her flowers and her lips or smelled her smell and imagined them coupling. It was hard to know the difference between normal and abnormal thoughts, and truthfully, he didn't care. Progenitor elimination would have to wait until after he secured Tanya's affections.

***

The Honda's slight pause in front of Tanya's duplex was long enough to alert Vic, who soon spotted the abandoned scooter. But, while New-Vic rounded the corner, Vic parked a few houses down and across the street, giving him a good, if diagonal, view of the place. The rustle of curtains on the left-side abode told him which half was hers.

***

New-Vic assumed he'd outwitted the Subaru and grabbed a space near the duplex. He crossed the lawn, spotting a planter filled with daisies. *Pretty*, he thought. *Not as pretty as her tattoo, but pretty*. He tore out a handful and fashioned them into a bouquet. They didn't smell sweet as flowers should, according to his olfactory memories of carnations around an old man's coffin.

***

"What the hell are you doing?" Vic mumbled, having half a mind to intercept the monster, although he knew warning Tanya would do nothing. He was mud in her eyes. And how do you explain to a gal that when she next sees you, she should ask you a specific agreed-upon question—with an agreed-upon answer—so she knows it's really you and not your double? Speaking of which, his double stood close to the duplex doors; deciding which door belonged to her.

***

New-Vic approached the door. So keyed up by the possibilities of this big moment. He knew enough to raise his voice so she'd hear him. "I'm 90 percent sure I'm falling in love with you. And I want you to forgive me and then fall in love with me, too."

Inside, Tanya listened, fear mingling with something she wasn't willing or ready to identify.

"I want to start over and do everything the proper way. I want you to tell me how."

Let's start with the naked good morning, Tanya thought.

"I close my eyes, and it's you I see." New-Vic pictured the hibiscus flowers entwined as lovers. "I hum a tune, and it's for you I sing."

Tanya frowned. Those words sounded rehearsed and lame.

"I don't know why I'm talking like a fool, Tanya. I guess I know an opportunity when I see one, and I don't want us to miss it." He rested his forehead on the door, circuits crackling with facts and memories that he wove into a courtship narrative. "Whatever story you want to write, I'll help if I can. Please trust me again."

She wasn't sure she ever quite did, but those were acceptable-enough words.

New-Vic stepped back at the sound of a beep and a bolt unlocking, his face bursting with joy as the door opened.

An older woman grinned at him. "Well, hello there, Romeo."

"I—I—I . . . " New-Vic didn't know how to finish so he thrust the daisies her way.

"I'll take 'em. Since they're technically mine, "but I think you want to be talking to her."

New-Vic followed her eyes, spinning around to find Tanya peeking out her half-opened door.

"That's a keeper, there," the woman said.

Tanya smiled, still ambivalent. "Millie, I'm going to call and check in with you in 20 minutes, yes?"

Millie nodded, a little less ebullient about burgeoning love as she closed her door.

New-Vic stepped forward as if Tanya were about to invite him inside. She placed her arm on the door frame instead.

"What happened to your eye?"

"I'd love to tell you about it over drinks."

"What makes you think you can stalker me home, steal my neighbor's flowers, and profess your love?" She didn't wait for an answer. "You don't know me well enough to be in love with me as a person. Maybe you're in love with a perception of who I am and who you think we could be. Or maybe I confused you by asking for your story. Because it was about the story. Maybe a minor flirtation, too, but the story was what—is what I want."

"But we interacted online," New-Vic said, mindscape a kaleidoscope of photos, status updates, quiz results, emojis, penises disappearing into train tunnels—"

"And you think that's the real me?"

"Bring on the meat?"

"God. You're a child."

"In many ways I am," New-Vic replied. "But like a child, I'm a quick and eager learner."

If she fell for this shit, if they got together and were married, and on some future anniversary when asked to recount their courtship, could she quote him with a straight face? "He won my heart by saying, 'like a child, I'm a quick and eager learner.'" Could she? She couldn't now. She could only laugh.

New-Vic joined her. "Ho-ho-no-hee-hee!"

As with pinkie fingers, goosebumps are vestigial remnants of a time when humans froze in caves and hunted by animals. Tanya's arms were riddled with them. "Why are you laughing that way?"

Uh oh. No. No. Did something wrong, New-Vic accessed files. *Ah,* Grey's Anatomy, *which progenitor will only admit to watching every single rerun if it gets him laid. It took a moment more, and then* he replaced his grin with a serious look. "Because I guess my default mode is 'horny asshole' who tries to ingratiate. Except you're too smart for that. People shouldn't underestimate you. I shouldn't underestimate you. I'm sorry."

"See, I know what you're doing. Admit to a wrong then flatter me," she said, stepping back like the conversation was over.

"How do I make it right?"

"First, tell me why you laughed that way."

New-Vic knew he must disavow her of the notion that he was an android the same as Stephan; most humans would never date one, or a half-and-half. Not yet, in any case.

"It was a stupid inside joke to myself," he said. "There's this android at LikeReal who has the same exact laugh, and I thought it was funny."

She searched his un-patched eye, hunting for glints of amber, but there was only a glossy affection. Her next question was about the eyepatch.

***

Vic, meanwhile, worried about two conflicting issues. First was Number One trapped in the Honda, and second, the Tanya-Clone tete-a-tete. Unable to focus on either, he chose a combination, scuttling down the street to crouch behind the Honda and watch the house, but resting the bandaged stump on the rear passenger window to comfort Number One, who was licking the glass. Lefty raised his phone and zoomed in for a picture of the clone at the door. CLICK.

Next was a close-up of his own stump with the clone in the background. CLICK. And then a selfie with the clone in the background. CLICK.

He remembered his extra key and darted to the front of the car, swiped his hand under the frame, and pulled out a key on a magnet. Except the key was missing. He'd left it in the junk drawer in the kitchen. *Fuck*.

He couldn't storm across the street—"unhand her, sir"—because to reveal the clone would assure their mutual destruction. An identical twin brother story might work for a while, but identical fingerprints in a world with speedy tech advancements and no birth certificate or ID for the clone? They'd both be living on borrowed time. Six months at best.

He glanced at his phone. Dead again. Number One whined. A hunger whine. Vic knew it well. He patted his jeans. *Who's got the wallet? Clone has the wallet. Perfect. No cash. No food for Number One. No phone.*

Norman came to the rescue, rather, the many memories of drunk Norman shoving Ritz Crackers in his mouth two at a time till he'd eaten a whole sleeve, and then complaining about his tongue's salt bloat. Norman always had a stash in his glove box.

Vic checked the other situation, worried about letting the parasitic abomination out of his sight. It was still at the front door but leaning against the frame, arms folded. They were embroiled in a heated conversation.

Oh God, if he goes in there. If he dates her. If he . . . loves her. If she loves him back. If they become a couple. If he's better than me. I'll die. I'll fucking die.

Could he leave for a minute? As an answer, Number One whimpered, his nails scrabbling on the window.

She's too strong a person to give in to him, he thought as he jogged down to the Subaru. He beeped it unlocked and rifled through Norman's glove box until he found a half-sleeve of Ritz.

"Is everything okay?" A woman's voice rang out behind him, the tone rhetorical, bordering on hostile.

Oh man, a nosy neighbor. Wait till I turn around and she gets a load of the patch and the scar.

"I'm fine, ma'am, just looking for my Ritz Crackers, which"—he turned to her, Lefty proffering the crackers— "I found in my glove box."

The woman, a stay-at-home trophy with an infant in a stroller and baby-weight boobs, would be easy to handle in Vic's estimation, and since she was already thrown off by the eyepatch, Vic seized the opportunity and added two statements:

"I'd offer you a cracker, but I can see you keep it healthy." And: "I'm a veteran."

They worked. Damn, they worked. She smiled in his

direction, mumbled a no-thank-you and a thank-you for his service, and resumed her jog.

Vic was 95 percent sure she wouldn't call the police and 75 percent sure that if she lived on this street, he'd be kept under surveillance. He sat on the hood, gnawing a stale cracker. Once she turned the corner, he hightailed it back to Number One.

Upon arrival, he saw both dog and clone were missing. And Tanya's door was motherfucking closed.

He stood there nibbling crackers for what might have been a half hour, long enough for jogging mom to return, rolling the baby-jogger up a driveway where she pulled out her phone, recording Vic as he stared at the duplex as though in a trance.

In truth, he was experiencing hunger of both the literal and sexual variety. If he kept the eye closed and concentrated on emptying his head, he felt almost palpable pangs. A cracker might quell a certain type of pang, but he needed a partner or a private space for the other. Was this symbiosis? *Are they doing it?*

A whirring sound broke his stupor. He crouched as a delivery drone descended, crossing Tanya's lawn to hover at her door. Chinese symbols adorned the packaging.

Oh no, Chinese food delivery. Did they do it already? Vic's modus operandi was always "sex before food makes the food taste good." But he shouldn't assume anything. Especially things that made him feel so hopeless.

***

A police drone—dubbed "Eyes in the Sky" by KTLA Channel 5's traffic reporter Audra del Sol—was two minutes out, having been dispatched from the NoHo station at the report of a prowler or perhaps a mental condition wandering through a neighborhood.

32

PLEASE BELIEVE ME

A TAXI PULLED UP next to the Subaru and deposited Stormin' Norman, wearing a twee ski cap with a pom-pom on top. "You're like the illegitimate bastard I fathered in tenth grade. Not that I, in fact, did." He beeped the Sube open. "But had I gotten into that sort of pickle? You, my friend, would be the result."

"Thanks, Dad." Vic wilted into the seat. "How'd you find us?"

"Lo-Jack sent me updates. Seems you've been at a yoga studio, and now . . . what's here, anyway?"

"My identical clone, probably rolling around naked on a floor full of fortune cookies. With my girl."

Norman nodded, thinking it best not to feed the pity monster today. Also not the time to inform him that his job was in jeopardy thanks to threatening Ralph, or how he'd been disinvited to the office picnic tomorrow. Of course Vic probably had no idea about the picnic in the first place since he spent company meetings doodling in his notebook.

"Do you have a charger for my Android?" Vic asked.

"No sir." Norman turned left at the corner, at the same moment the police drone arrived to find nothing amiss.

Vic kept quiet the entire trip and didn't respond when Norman quoted Seneca: "We suffer more in imagination than in reality."

Upon arrival at La Villa Armada, Norman accompanied

Vic inside. Why? Why? Because Norman was a damned enabler, which was why Pam went feral-bitch on him. He never said, "hey this narcissistic, hysterical, emasculating diva nonsense shall not pass." He played victim, irking her enough to seek sexual comfort elsewhere. *Yep, I'm a helper*, he brooded.

Vic had still said nothing by the time they entered his apartment. His response to Norman's slow whistle at the punched-in wall, blood spatter, and evidence of rampage was plugging his phone into the charger.

Norman found a non-bloody spot on the couch and sat, quietly watching Vic stare at the phone. Minutes went by.

"Where's Number One?" Norman asked.

Nothing.

What was a guy to do but sit quietly? Norman's psychological knowledge extended as far as couples' therapy, in which he was always cast as a catalyst, and books on psychological tactics for people managers who wanted to forge productive relationships with their subordinates. Now, thanks to Vic, he could add a new branch to his knowledge tree: Xenomelia, the desire to be disabled that can result in self-amputation. Is this what Vic wanted? It normally began in adolescence. He remembered a story Vic told him about the time he lanced a skin tag on his inner thigh using his Swiss Army knife. Come to think of it, it was Paps he sliced at Paps's request. A little hydrogen peroxide stopped the bleed, and the wart never came back. No, wait, it did, but Paps hid it from him. But it was only half-formed. *For cryin' out loud, what have I become? I have my own problems.* Norman clutched his head. *After this, we're square, little buddy. Two weeks on a couch is a pittance next to this calamity.*

Another five minutes passed. Norman was speculating on whether Vic had developed a drug or alcohol habit, when Vic unplugged his phone and walked it over to Norman, shoving it close to his face. "Tell me, what is this?"

"A photo of you talking to, I'm going to guess, Tanya?"

"Who's the guy?"

"You."

"Who took the picture?"

"I don't know, bud."

"I did. I took the picture, and that's not me."

"Looks like you."

"Now this." Vic showed him a photo with the same angle and subjects, but with the bandaged stump in the foreground.

"Still you."

"How did I hold the camera and take a picture of my hand up close and myself 30 yards away?"

"I don't know, maybe you used that Adobe app—"

"Check it." This image was a Vic-selfie, with the other Vic in the background at the door.

"Still the Adobe app the—"

"Nope.

Norman rubbed the top of his ski cap, an inkling of dread, a boatload of confusion.

"It grew into a version of me."

"What did?"

"The hand. The missing fucking hand, Norman." Vic stomped to his bedroom. "Follow me, please." Despite his better judgment he followed. "Check this out." Vic crouched next to his bed and pulled up the comforter so Norman could see the cereal bowls. "See?"

"Yes."

"Now look at this." Vic slid the closet open, pointed to the chicken bones in the golf shoes. "Well?"

Norman shrugged. "Logic dictates that you put the bowls under the bed and the bones in the shoe. At the time, you must have had a reason—"

"How about this, then?" Vic scrolled through recent texts, found Tanya's, and called her. "I'm calling Tanya, who is at this moment with me in her house doing God knows what." He thrust the cell at Norman. "When she answers, ask to speak to Vic."

Norman backed away, hands up. "Enough, Vic, really."

"Fine!" He switched it to speaker, holding it so Norman could hear, too.

Tanya's "hello" was faint. Still, Vic's heart fluttered, not like a happy bird, but a bird who's sure its mate unwittingly betrayed it with another.

"Hi, can I speak to Vic?" Vic asked.

"Uh . . . sure . . . "

Vic turned up the in-call volume.

His own voice said, "Is this who I think it is?"

Vic pulled the phone closer to his mouth. "If you think it's the real Vic Moss who's going to kill you, then yeah, it's who you think it is."

CLICK.

Norman staggered out to the couch. All those years spent devouring Bradbury and Asimov, Wells, Huxley, Heinlein, Clarke, Gaiman, Ellison and Le Guin had not prepared him for his own science fiction tribulation. He groped for quotes, for any logical explanation to understand what was happening, but found nothing except a ridiculous science fiction premise of which he found himself a participant, entangled in an objective reality few humans had ever experienced.

Vic sat beside him, turned on the TV. *Family Feud.* This television rarely patronized any channels other than the Game Show Network and porn.

Two shows later, the Hornberger family had amassed 12 grand in winnings, and Norman and Vic were dozing on the couch. Vic's dreams incorporated sounds from the show. " . . . you better not talk that way to your wife, or you *will* feel the burn," Steve Harvey said.

"Pencils!" cried a contestant. Vic awoke to the sounds of buzzers, and shot to his feet, with an idea roaring through his head.

The movement roused Norman. "What's happening? What time is it?"

"Hey, tomorrow can you pick me up at 9:30 in the morning?"

"Tomorrow is bad."

"Bring the kid, it'll be fast."

"No kid this weekend. It's the picnic, remember?"

Vic's blankness told him no.

"Apparently, you threatened Chet, so . . . ."

"Not me."

"Whomever."

Another worry to add to Vic's list, but it would have to wait since the only important matter was remaining the only Vic Moss in existence. "What time does the picnic start?"

"Between 10 and 11."

"We'll be done by then."

"I'm driving Amy and Sunil, so . . . ."

"They can help."

"HR issues I do not need, and you, especially, do not need."

"They can wait in your car! It's an in-out-bang-boom type of deal. It's my only chance. You saw the pictures! You heard the voice. It sat at my desk. Please, Norman! This must end."

Norman pictured the two different t-shirts Vic wore today. The disjointed conversations he'd had with each Vic. The voice on the phone. The photos. It was real, and it did nothing to assuage his fears about a machine takeover.

"Norman." Vic snapped his fingers. "Please."

Potential career destruction aside, part of him ached to participate in a science fiction narrative he'd dreamed of as a child, masturbated about in his teens, and ruminated upon as an adult. Another part of him felt helpless to say "no" to this sad bastard. No man should have to compete with his own clone, for cryin' out loud!

"In-out-bing-bang-boom?"

Vic wrapped him in a grateful hug.

33.

GETTING TO GO-TIME

THE MARCH 15, 1985 *Los Angeles Times* headline read: *Play Ball! Boys Win Right to Play on Little League Softball Teams!* Decades later, this superior court ruling allowed a young Vic entry to Harrold's Carpets, the Harrold's Carpets-sponsored girls' team, as a second baseman. Which is also how far he got with left field, first base, right field, and shortstop. Pitcher was gay. Catcher, too scary. Center field and third base were out of his league. As for the benchwarmers, he'd slid to third with most of them.

Alas, his reign of groping ended when the girls discovered baseball boys, and Vic morphed into Milhouse Van Houten, worshipping them from afar but ignored unless called upon to provide ego-bolstering insight into the psyche of young teenage boys. The girls would ask, "Does Tobias/Tom/Tony/Thomas/Tray/Tristan like me? Or *like-me* like me?" Even at 13, he knew the Good Ship Vic was drifting on bad winds to rocky shores, and he'd better seize the wheel before it was too late.

This early realization steered him to the Way of the Sword, and by the time the softball girls had gotten their hearts broken by the baseball boys, Vic was studying with a sensei and owned a stellar katana, which was now stowed in his belted sheath attached to his denim shorts as he stood outside the gates of the Villa Armada, awaiting Norman.

Also included in his ensemble was a Louisville Slugger, purchased after leaving the girls' team, and hoping to try out for baseball, which he never did, because the swords happened, and they were everything. He usually kept it tucked between his bed and the wall, but today Lefty held it. Righty wore a mitt, secured to the stump by the remains of his duct tape.

Norman arrived at 9:36. He wore a baseball cap with the JMS company logo. *Fucking middle-management suck-up,* Vic thought. *And six minutes late.* Amy and Sunil looked like sleep-deprived kittens slumped in the back seat.

"You playing baseball today?" Norman asked, eyeing the Louisville Slugger.

"Crackin' a few balls, yep."

"Do not get into this car with the sword."

"Really?"

"You can't walk around with a sword unless you're on a convention floor. I'll allow the bat since 'going to the park' is a believable excuse should the police spot you walking around this way, a grown man."

"We're late, though!"

"Then hurry."

Vic stomped his feet like a teenage girl before rushing back to his apartment. Round-trip took two minutes. He got in the front passenger seat, turning around to nod to the pair in back. "Happy picnic day."

Amy was sound asleep. Sunil, without a laptop, seemed surreal. Sunil speaking more than a dozen words in one spell was unprecedented.

"There will be a bounce house," Sunil said. "I love the bounce houses. You should not eat before you go into the bounce house. There will also be a bubble suit that allows you to throw yourself on the ground and bounce back up to standing."

"Sounds fun." Vic put on his own seat belt. Norman gave him an approving nod. "You'd better haul ass,

Skipper, cuz if we're not there by ten sharp," he switched to a whisper, "I'm fucking dead."

"Coordinates," said Norman.

On my phone, get to Chinatown and then we'll go east. We have 18 minutes, but the map says 21.

"We'll get there." Norman cranked up some classic Timberlake for the ride.

As they chugged down Interstate 5, Norman switched the music to blast in back and mute in front. "What are we doing?"

Vic laid out the scheme as he'd done that morning in his *Killing It* goals . . .

1: Wait for Trash Robot to emerge from his door and roll halfway across the alley.

2: Norman, thin and flexible for an old dude, enters building via the robot door.

3: Vic hides the bat down the back of his cargo shorts; gains entry through the front door, at which point . . .

4: Vic either gets past Stephan amicably or uses the slugger.

4-A: Circumvent Doctor Cord. Take him down if necessary.

5: Norman opens the lab door for Vic from the inside. They find and deploy the kill switch.

During last night's *Family Feud*, the buzzer had dislodged a memory of the kill switch/kill button Cord mentioned when Vic asked him how a prosthesis might be deactivated. Cord's eyes had flitted towards his lab. Hence, the kill switch/button was in the lab, and God help Vic if it didn't kill full-blown clones.

6: If necessary, threaten Cord with a major lawsuit and publicity.

6-A: Incorporate Tanya's article into the mix, regaining her affection.

***

At 9:56, Norman parked in the alley, 10 yards beyond Cord's dumpster, presumably out of camera range. Vic turned to Sunil. "We're going inside for a little bit, so you sit in the driver's seat and move the Sube if a truck comes by."

Sunil looked at him blankly, his mind already in the bounce house.

"Can you drive?" Vic asked.

"In theory, yes," Sunil said.

"Good enough." Everyone but sleeping Amy got out of the car. Sunil got into the driver's seat. Norman's face clouded with vexation as Sunil adjusted the seat and mirrors.

"If we come out fast, start the car," Vic explained. "We'll jump in back, and you gun it down the alley."

"Are you robbing a bank?" Sunil asked.

"No, but the guy in there is crazy, so I don't know what to expect. All *you* have to do is get us out of here, then you can pull over and Norman will drive. Can you handle that?"

Sunil eyeballed the control panel. "Yes."

"This isn't Balboa Park." Amy was awake.

"Good morning, star shine," Vic said. "To catch you up, there's gonna be a little robot coming out that little door, and rolling across the alley to the dumpster—"

"No way," Norman said. "She's an intern."

"Should I lie to her? She's gonna see things, Norman."

"I was not informed of robots," Sunil said.

"Now you are. It's tiny. You're not afraid of a tiny robot, are you, Sunil?"

"In theory, no."

Norman shook his head. "It's an HR issue waiting to happen."

Vic ignored him. "It's going to dump a garbage cube into the dumpster, then it'll turn around and roll back through its door."

"Ohhhhh . . . kay," she said, eyes gauging Norman, who wore the resigned look her dad used to get when once upon many times he accompanied her to princess birthday parties.

"Your job is to set it off track," Vic said.

"Still no," Norman said without conviction.

Amy rubbed the sleep out of her eyes, blinked at Vic. "You say it's tiny, how tiny?"

"Too short to ride a roller coaster."

She looked up at Norman again. "I want sixteen credited hours for this."

Norman nodded weakly.

"I'll fuck its shit up."

Norman threw his hands up in the air. "If she gets hurt, we get sued, the company gets sued—"

"She won't get hurt," Vic said, then to Amy, "wait until it drops its trash load; it'll be lighter."

All one-hundred pounds of Amy sprung out of the car. "Super Swiss Army unite." She extended her arm with the knife bracelet on her wrist. Lefty pulled out his dog tag/Swiss Army necklace and they toasted.

Randomly exploring the car, Sunil gave a startled outcry when the windshield wipers activated.

Norman slapped his forehead. "Sunil! Don't push buttons."

Sunil nodded, put both hands back on the wheel.

"Okay. We're all set." Vic checked his watch: 9:59. Almost time! He motioned Amy to take position to the side of the dumpster and for Norman to press himself against the wall by the robot door. Vic himself slid the Kansas City slugger down the back of his shirt, into his cargo shorts and tighty-whities.

Once in position, everyone threw everyone a thumbs-up, even to Sunil, wearing the frightened face of a high schooler awaiting his first driving lesson.

30 seconds crept by in silence, except for their beating hearts. An electronic humming like auto-tuned bees sounded. The robot's door slid open. Trash Robot emerged, holding a compacted trash cube in its pincers.

"Go-time," Vic said.

34.
KILL-SWITCH

ON VIC'S SIGNAL: Norman flipped his baseball cap backward and crawled through the open robot door; Amy stood next to the dumpster, bouncing from foot to foot like a boxer waiting for the bell; Sunil looked horrified.

Vic sprinted to the front door, where he addressed the camera: "Hello, brother, it's Save-the-Date day." He knocked insistently with both Lefty and The Mitt.

***

Norman slithered inside the lab, unsettled by the vehemence of Vic's far-off knocking.

***

Vic continued his barrage. "Sorry I didn't RSVP, but I'm here. Stephan? Doctor Cord?"

***

As Trash Robot rolled closer to the dumpster, Amy froze statue-still in case it had movement sensors. Last year she'd contributed language parameters to a classmate's AI, a hybrid of Roomba and Siri, so she was aware of the AIs' general capabilities but in no way prepared for its top half telescoping up four feet. Seized by a sudden prescience of doom, she yelped. Once the trash cube dropped into the dumpster, Trash Robot pivoted, enveloping Amy within its shadow.

***

Norman's eyes adjusted and raked the place . . . Bunsen burners, banks of computer lights stacked up a wall . . . a dentist's chair? At his left hip stood a sturdy metal desk, and a man in a chair slumped over the desk. Norman strained his ears past the endless knocking and picked out the thick breaths of slumber. Alive. Norman plied south, ballerina-style, until his head disappeared below desk-level.

The knocking stopped. Norman inhaled. The man snorted awake.

"Stephan?" The man rolled away from the desk.

Norman curled up like a roly-poly bug, exhaling ever so slowly.

***

The front doors whooshed open to a smiling Stephan blocking entry.

"Are you gonna let me pass, Stephan?" This was the first and only time Vic correctly pronounced his name.

***

Trash Robot wrapped its pincers around Amy's chest, picked her up and shook her. She yelped, rag dolling, feet kicking. Every kick made her heavier, got her closer to the ground. Finally, her high-tops touched concrete. Then again. This time she pushed off the ground, throwing all her weight against the robot body and careening in reverse until it clanked against the dumpster. The pincers slackened and Amy threw herself forward out of its grasp.

***

"I will be happy to let the doctor know you're here," were Stephan's last words before Lefty withdrew the bat from its underpants sheath and brought it down on Stephan's head with extreme prejudice. Stephan sank to his knees. The dent on his noggin gave the head a grotesque heart shape. But Stephan still wore that unctuous smile—his last smile—until Vic roundhoused with the bat, slugging the android's jaw so hard his teeth tore through the other side of his face.

Stephan dispatched, check. He stepped over the crumpled body.

***

The robot wheeled after Amy, its exoskeleton shooting out yet another foot, pincers clicking at her. One caught a braid and dragged her off her feet. Her hands clung to the pincers to reduce hair pull, bracelet dangling wildly. The bracelet! She released a hand in order to unfold the Swiss Army knife, feeling hair ripping away from her scalp. "Ow! You big bastard!" She sawed at the braid, until it fell clean off and her body dropped from the pincers' grip. As soon as she hit the ground, she shot to her feet.

Sunil screamed. His hands gripped the wheel. He had to pee.

Badass Amy was running to the car, and the robot followed fast. But wait! All of a sudden, she about-faced, rushing straight at the thing, evading its pincers like a ninja gymnast. When she got close enough, she suddenly dropped into a kneeling position with her head tucked. Her opponent crashed into her and toppled straight over onto its back.

***

Norman, still roly-poly'd, dared a glance up at the man in the lab coat, shuffling across the room. Unfortunately, sounds drifting through the open robot door—an engine revving . . . Amy yelling, "Man up, Sunil!"—caught the man's ear and he stopped, cocking his head. "Kill it already!"

"Garble!" the man cried.

***

"Kill it, kill it, kill it," cried one-braid Amy, sitting shotgun in the Sube, which Sunil still had in Park.

Trash robot turtled around on its back trying to build momentum to stand upright again.

"It will be as though we hit a giant metal deer," Sunil whined. "I cannot be responsible for damage to Norman's car."

"If that thing gets up, this car is toast anyway." Sunil's quavering finger pushed the ignition button. Amy said. "And so are we." He revved the engine.

***

On the way down the hallway, Vic paused to whack the automaton head off its display mount, then continued his journey to the lab, hoping Norman would be able to get those doors open fast, cuz his ass was *not* slowing down. Behind him, the automaton said in a loop: "Danger, Kenny Cord, Danger, Kenny Cord . . . "

***

The thought of an early mortality filled Sunil with rage strong enough to vanquish the full-body trembling and transform him into a cold-blooded killer whose weapon was a family sedan. He gunned the Subaru down the alley at tire-shredding speed culminating in a head-on collision with Trash Robot. He and Amy screamed on impact. Air bags deployed.

A moment of stunned silence preceded the popping and shredding noises as Amy deflated the airbags enough for them to see Trash Robot's smashed up head and distended torso.

"Dayam, Sunil. You are an ass-kicking freak!"

"And you are quite frightening!"

***

Doctor Cord drifted back toward the desk, eyes wide and flickering amber at the faint sounds of the car tooting its horn. His Crocs halted a toe's length from the checkered Vans belonging to the man squatting by Garble's door.

"Who are you?" asked Cord—rather, New-Cord. He pulled off Norman's baseball cap. The baldness startled him a few steps back, creating an opening for Norman to drive forward, spindly arms beating in front of him like a demented hand blender.

***

"You did good," Amy said.

"I wanted it to suffer," Sunil admitted.

During this moment of triumph, they failed to see the shambling man with the amber eyes until he leaped on the hood and slammed a can of creamed corn against the already riddled windshield.

"Go!" Amy yelled. Sunil went. The force of acceleration pressed the guy against the windshield, leaving Sunil with a small view between his legs. Up top, the droid held onto the luggage rack, swinging around to kick the driver's side window until it cracked.

"Oh no! Oh no!" Sunil wailed, veering left then right, but the guy held on, and every bump and swerve sent his boot banging into the window until glass shards sprayed the interior. "I will scrape him into the wall!" Sunil steered to the alley's edge.

The man swung himself back to the center of the windshield a split-second before the Subaru edged the wall. A keening sound of the door handle scraping against concrete sent chills up Amy and Sunil's spines. Sunil adjusted right, tearing up to 50 MPH, to 60, to 65, then stomped the brake. The guy's body arced from car to sky to concrete and landed with an awful thud, head turned completely around. His black eyes stared up at the sky.

"He attacked us first," Amy said.

***

The lab doors opened as Vic neared! He didn't even need to reduce speed.

Cord and Norman's slap fight had evolved into a full-on wrestling match. Vic stepped over a discarded Croc and broken glass, circling the duo, waiting for a clear shot. Cord's hands throttled Norman's chicken neck, creating an opening and BOOM went the bat upside Cord's head. He collapsed on top of Norman.

Vic kicked the body off and helped Norman to his feet. "Did you just kill a man, little buddy?"

Vic's teeth chattered in the rush of adrenaline. Had the medications and fear and sadness transmogrified into a cockamamie conspiracy theory resulting in a man's death?

LIKE REAL

Was it all in his head? Norman repeated the question, but all Vic could manage for a response was dropping the bat.

"Wait. Look at this," Norman said. "At the eyes."

Although neither had seen the open eyes of a dead man outside of the movies they knew these were abnormal. If Vic sustained any religious paranoia, he'd say these were the black eyes of a demon.

Norman jumped away from the seeping blood. "It's pink for cryin' out loud. Is he another . . . ?"

"Best not speculate," Vic said.

"Touché." Norman nudged the dead man with his shoe, then remembered. "Buttons!"

"Right, buttons." Vic pointed at the desk. "I think they deactivate the prostheses, which . . . I guess these things are the grown-up versions of."

"They're labeled. Must be initials." Norman squinted as he drew closer. He patted his pockets, found his dollar store readers. Damn things had thumb prints on the lenses.

A moment ago, the melee of the fight and ensuing shock had covered the whoosh of the lab's doors. By the time Norman and Vic discovered that someone had crept into the lab, acquired a weapon and was bearing down on them, New-Vic was within spitting distance.

Vic heard the crunch of glass. Behind him. It was inevitable, wasn't it? He turned to find the Vic clone holding the Kansas City slugger by the wrong end. Still menacing, though. He took a step forward. CRUNCH.

"Stop. Stop for a second," Vic commanded. New-Vic obeyed. "Answer a question. I have to know. Did you, with Tanya? Did you . . . ?"

"Yeah, it was a trip to the moon and back."

"You're lying."

New-Vic accessed Vic's memories, adjusted the bat so he held it properly.

Norman, who'd frozen when the clone spoke, risked movement, pushing a button at random.

***

JB, aka Jimmy, aka Jim Brooker, borderline sociopath who'd lost half his leg in a motorcycle accident as a teenager, steered his golf cart in the direction of the ninth hole. Upon deactivation, his eyes shuttered to black, and his limp body teetered as the cart put-putted down a slight hill into the tree line. Although the impact was gentle, the body flopped onto the grass.

***

New-Vic accessed a montage of Vic memories about people on TV explaining their deeds to a captive—sometimes literally—audience, and, figuring this was required, he recounted his experience. Tanya tried to interview him. He'd been cagey. She ordered food and shared it with him. He liked the egg rolls but did not enjoy hot mustard. It hurt his nose. They drank sake, which made him tired, so he fell asleep on her couch—apparently clones sleep, too—and then Vic had called.

"What did you tell her?"

"Not much. I love her."

"Did you tell her that?"

"Of course."

"What? Idiot! Why did you go so fast? She'll think you're a dope—"

"Don't give him tips, for cryin' out loud," Norman cut in.

"Why did all of this even happen? Why did *you* happen? You were a damn hand, not even a whole hand!"

New-Vic knew there wasn't time to relay the information he'd received from the Phantasm 8, plus there was the problem of Norman bending over the desk. "Step away from there, Skipper."

It was wrong, so wrong that the clone knew this nickname. Before turning around to the two Vics, Norman pushed a button labeled *JY*.

***

JY, aka Sergeant Joan, aka Captain Jennifer Young, aka New-Captain Jennifer, was taking a dip in the pool while the children and the husband observed from a patio table full of empty breakfast dishes. They had encouraged her to eat and then swim, as if she hadn't accessed safety information on swimming, one of the warnings being not to do so after eating for fear of dissolved gases becoming bubbles inside the body on depressurization. Ergo, they wished her harm. Upon deactivation, she sank. The family quietly watched the body disappear and then pop to the surface and bob lifelessly. Nobody moved or said a word.

***

Back in the lab, New-Vic ordered Norman to put his hands up, "Where I can see them"—a phrase culled from Vic's memories of cowboy movies. It sounded appropriately stern as it rolled off his tongue.

"Are you going to kill me?" Vic said. "And him? And the people outside? Is this going turn into a murder spree?"

"You threatened to chop me to pieces!"

Still backing away from swing distance, Vic said, "What was supposed to happen? How were you going to . . . happen?"

"Gradual assimilation."

"So, devour Vic Moss from the inside?"

"Co-existence. A better existence. The cycle wouldn't have been interrupted, and I wouldn't have had to grow up alone in a closet."

"So all this is my fault?"

"It's not *my* fault!"

"Your very first act as a sentient being was to show your dick to my date—"

"I didn't understand; I didn't ask for any of this—"

"You keep pushing my buttons. Bang, bang!"

"I didn't ask to be. I didn't know anything until you made me—"

"You keep pressing my buttons like in *Family Feud*, bang, bang, bang!"

Norman finally sussed the meaning and dropped an arm to the desk, fingers spidering to the buttons.

"Stop confusing me!" New-Vic advanced, bat cocked and quivering.

"Norman!" Vic yelled. The clone glanced over as Norman pushed the last two un-deployed buttons.

"You do not end me, motherfucker," New-Vic bellowed. "I end you!"

***

HH, aka Hank, aka Henry Hatch, aka New-Henry Hatch, seated at the crowded counter in the Glendale Galleria food court, simply dropped his chin. The high-backed plastic chair kept him seated, so he appeared to be praying over his bowl of salmon poke.

***

New-Vic collapsed in mid-swing, the bat inches from Vic's noggin.

"Couldn't see the letters," Norman said. "Gotta get some wipes."

The honking outside, which began as polite beeps, had escalated to prolonged bleating. Vic collected the bat, and he and Norman hustled out. The sound of the automaton intoning "Danger, Kenny Cord . . . ." increased the spook factor tenfold for Norman, as did the sight of Stephan's heart-head and cheek-teeth. He couldn't get out the front door fast enough.

Vic stopped short before crossing the threshold. "You go ahead; give me a minute."

"What are you doing?"

"I'll be right back."

Norman, dog-tired, face raked by clone fingernails, the last 200 hairs on his head a tangle of fraying braid, patted Vic's shoulder and vamoosed, certain he'd be arrested for aiding and abetting destruction of property. Upon rounding the corner of the warehouse, he saw the state of his vehicle and sank to his knees. "Oh, for cryin' out loud . . . "

***

Vic barreled through the lobby, down the hallway, pausing to kick the automaton's head until it spoke no more, then into the lab to his first goal: the front left pocket of Clone-Vic's jeans pocket where Vic was certain he kept his keys. *His* goddamned keys. *His* goddamned wallet. Bingo! He set off again, stopping briefly at the surgery chair to snatch the folded blanket on its seat, and back into the reception area for goal number two: the suit of armor. Too rad to leave behind. He prayed for strength as he jostled all 50 pounds of it off the mount and foisted it up on his shoulder, fireman-style. He almost tripped over Stephan on his way out.

Waking Stephan up.

***

Norman shook his head when Vic emerged with the suit of armor. "No, sir, I do not need scuff marks on the roof."

Vic almost laughed at the irony of Norman worrying about his roof when the rest of his car was a horror show. "Skipper." He pointed his key fob towards the front of the building, where his Honda beeped unlocked. "I just need some rope."

Norman popped his trunk, handed over a coil of thin rope. "I'm a fucking helper," he said.

"I love you."

"Fuck off." Norman shook his head. "Sorry. I know you'll pay for all the damage." He pointed his finger at Vic for emphasis. "Sunil, I'm driving, get out of the front seat."

Vic trudged to the Fit, leaning the suit of armor against the trunk so he could have both arms free for his reunion with Number One, who was zipping from window to window, whining for his buddy. Vic cried in gratitude. His baby boo-boo honey boy was okay.

35.

FIXES

VIC BOUGHT AMY an expensive haircut, and Sunil front-of-line admission to the Human Slingshot up by Fresno. To Norman he vowed that all drama was behind him, and he'd give at least 90 percent at work from then on. Chet got a profuse apology. Vic cited mental issues due to his catastrophic amputation and casually referenced a lawyer. He kept his job, but only 2,500 shares instead of 10,000. He also began adapting to a non-sentient prosthesis.

***

"Tell us why you chose a minimally tested next-generation prosthesis in the first place, and did you even know you were a test subject?" Tanya asked Vic. She was speaking into her brand-new WAD Audio MixDown X5 studio microphone.

"Well, nobody mentioned the FDA or the American Medical Association, but all the equipment, and the people who'd had it done before, looked good, and the parts looked real," Vic answered in a computer-altered voice.

From outside the aluminum-sided storage shed, the only sign of a fringe radio/internet show recording session was a large antenna on its roof. Tanya was becoming a popular voice in the paranormal and ufology community, with 1800-something dedicated listeners in Los Angeles County and another 600-700 scattered through Kern and

194

San Bernardino Counties, not to mention YouTube followers numbering in the five figures and rising.

Vic told his story from start to finish. At her behest, he didn't identify the company by name. Tanya didn't need a lawsuit or a reunion with the robot receptionist.

Tanya chimed in here and there, citing the moment she realized the full scope of the situation when she got a phone call from "Dean Winger" while another "Dean Winger" was standing next to her, and how the guy in her living room had eyes that didn't seem altogether human. She'd simply walked out her front door, gotten onto her Vespa, and driven up to Bakersfield for a few days until certain he'd cleared out of her apartment.

Vic, aware of her disinterest in any romance rekindling, was pleased she'd chosen to interview him rather than see him prosecuted. Still miffed about her maybe hooking up with clone-boy, he outright asked her whether anything untoward went down.

Tanya explained her interest in him was for an interview, nothing more, as if she even needed to explain it to this guy. Even without the hand-clone issues, Vic was trouble, and she was done with troubled lads—at least the ones who lived in their cars or who made idiotic decisions such as getting a body part replacement from a deranged scientist.

She paid him in cookies and a hundred-dollar bill and made ten times as much in sponsored ads. This was a good thread to pull for years to come and might even be fodder for a memoir. The paranormal community came with a lot of disposable incomes and an unceasing thirst for content.

The experience with Vic also taught her that the great American journalism she'd yearned to write—culture pieces about the Bauhaus Movement, interviews with avant-garde songwriters and filmmakers, political essays from the feminist perspective—wasn't for her. She'd been a Nightstalker type all along, mining the zeitgeist for oddities, unidentified aerial phenomena, and paranormal conspiracies. This was her milieu, and she reveled in it.

She never once missed Cindy, now the editor-in-chief of the entertainment beat, and especially didn't miss Conner, although she was forced to think about him once in a while when one of his articles tickled the scrotums of many 20-something douches who hailed him as a gonzo god. This dipshit dropped acid and spent the weekend on a soundstage with holographic depictions of the dead and famous, including Tupac, Maria Callas, Mamie Van Doren and Teddy Roosevelt. The article, titled "A Holographic Hootenanny in LSD-Flat," relayed Conner's experience of watching Teddy shoot guns in the air wild-west style and what it's like to wear adult diapers for a 24-hour trip-out. It was self-aggrandizing, scatological nonsense, yet many dubbed him the Hunter S. of his generation—minus political satire or genuine talent.

She wondered—but did not ask for fear of giving Conor a shout-out on her show—if Vic had also seen the article, and if so, had he drawn a similar conclusion as Connor about how they were lucky to be alive at the dawn of holographic immersion similar to the Holodeck on *Star Trek: TNG?* In ten years, Vic could cosplay as Riker at the jazz club, or Data in Victorian London—two examples Connor referenced, the fucker. Hell, Vic could fight Klingons with his katanas.

***

It took a few weeks for Vic's work suspension to end and for the apartment to look almost good as new. An art restoration place repaired the Hoo Maru, and Vic paid for new carpet, plastering and paint. Sizzling with goals and running at a solid 85 percent, he had two more days until he went back to work.

On Saturday morning, Cozy knocked on his door to inform him that at noon exactly, she was, "going to swim from one end of the pool and back without a floaties or a life jacket!" If he cared to watch, they were barbecuing ribs afterward.

Vic smiled. "I knew you could do it." She spun girlishly

in his praise. He noticed the diamond on her finger and she spun some more because, yes! She and Jun-ho were engaged. All this time, Vic thought she was his sidepiece when he came to town for business.

"Bravo!" he said with a gusto he didn't feel, and hugged her, not even perving upon boob contact—*not* because he'd grown as a human, nay, but because a few minutes prior to her visit, he'd opened the linen closet for some fresh pillowcases and found a cereal bowl with a bit of milk still in it hidden under the hand towels.

Which meant the clone was back. Somehow.

He promised to be at her swimming debut, offered a Norman-flavored platitude about perseverance, then closed his door and ran pell-mell through his house, opening doors and cupboards, locking windows, pulling off his sheets, stabbing the shower curtain. Where was that fucker hiding? Did it intend to kill and replace him? How did it resurrect itself?

***

It had taken Stephan a good 20 minutes to reboot. Systems were weak. Head bashed. Skin pierced by teeth. Limited visibility of simple shapes and colors. And only one ManChine could fix him. He rolled to his belly, hands clawing the zebra carpet as he pulled his torso and inoperative legs behind him. Almost an hour passed before he made it through the reception lounge, down the hall and to the lab.

The doors opened; Stephan inched inside, trailing past ManChine Cord lying spread-eagled in a landscape of blood and broken glass. In another few minutes, he got to the desk, grasping its metal top with both hands for a slow chin-up until he could rest on his elbows. Then he pushed all the buttons back to active.

First, ManChine Henry woke up in the food court, thronging with hungry shoppers. His poke stunk. The Food Court janitor nudged him with his broom handle. "Thank you, kind person. I fell into a nap," ManChine Henry said.

The Janitor nodded guardedly, the way one does when dealing with a drunk.

Next, ManChine Jennifer, whose body had been corralled by the current of the pool cleaner into a corner of the shallow end, sputtered and kicked back to life. Jennifer's family watched grim-faced from behind the sliding glass door of the kitchen as she crawled up the pool stairs and vomited a gallon of water on the deck.

ManChine Jim, spread-eagled on the greens, opened his eyes. Instead of the trees and sky, several male faces stared down on him. As he sat up, he recognized their attire—golf casual shorts and a polo, the chic whites of a country club doctor, the third guy in a security uniform. Jim had totaled the cart and wounded a tree.

ManChines Cord and Victor sat up behind Stephan.

"All back online," Stephan hissed through the gash that used to be his mouth. He collapsed.

ManchineCord scooped him up, cradling him like the Pietà as he examined the damage. "You will fix me," Stephan whispered.

"I will fix you."

36.
FEINTING

ALL SWORDS WERE gone from their displays. How long had this cohabitation been going on? The lone cereal bowl suggested a single day. And in this slice of time, the clone had thought to purloin the weapons? Even the suit of armor, displayed in a corner on a stand, was missing its battle ax. Vic knew his time must be short.

Careful not to think too hard about a plan, lest the strange symbiotic sensory thing was still happening, Vic whistled as he harnessed Number One, grabbed his keys and phone, and focused on a pleasant drive down into the Valley. Hopefully, the thing wasn't too attuned with the environment yet, or it would know a trip deeper into the Valley was rarely pleasant. On the drive to Norman's, he plotted the perfect move to permanently disable that fucker.

Feinting was a sword fighting technique in which a fighter provoked the enemy into making a mistake or lunging too quickly, allowing the fighter to attack first. In his swordplay with Proto, neither the term for this technique nor any of its tenets had come to mind, nor was it a recent memory. So, it might work.

Norman had custody of Hanna this weekend, and both were getting ready for a World Series game when Vic arrived, asking to borrow a few things.

"You promised no more drama."

"This is it, Skipper, I swear."

Norman couldn't risk an argument in the presence of his baby girl, who might bring a story home to Pam. "Take what you need, little buddy, then go."

Vic nodded, mumbled a thanks. On his way out the door, Norman called out, "An eye for an eye only makes the whole world blind . . . " Vic shut the door as Norman said, "Gandhi."

***

Jun-ho, Yeon-jin, Cozy, Mamie and a few tenants buzzed with excitement down by the pool. The fellas heated the barbecue, adding hickory wood chips to the charcoal. Mamie huddled with Cozy, giving her a pep talk.

It was 32 years to the day since Cozy almost drowned trying and failing to save their sister Hildy from a riptide off the Santa Barbara coast. Cozy whispered to Mamie, "I'm doing this for her." The sisters touched foreheads, remembering "Momma's sweet surprise," who would have turned 40 this month.

Cozy waded into the shallow end. Everyone clapped as she took her first strokes and hoorayed as she treaded water without panic or a life preserver.

Vic pattered upstairs unnoticed. He wore Norman's 44-inch-long sword with its straight, double-edged blade in a sheath, and carried a big roll of duct tape—way more than anyone but an electrician or a psychopath might need. He fashioned a duct tape sheath to the wall on the other side of the front door, smoothing it as tight as it could get against the stucco, then inserted the sword, careful that its sharp double edges didn't slice through.

***

Inside the bedroom, New-Vic gripped the steel katana, listening to the front door open. He'd cracked the bedroom door enough so he could kick it open with a bang but not enough so the dog would come in and bug him. He sure hoped the dog would steer clear when the sword began its deadly business.

"Hello?" New-Vic tensed at hearing his own voice. "You came back, didn't you?" New-Vic stayed quiet, even as the bedroom door nudged open and the dog squeezed through.

"No, baby, not right now," New-Vic whispered to the mutt, who nose-bumped his leg until New-Vic scratched his head. The newer hand, fully formed now, looked as real as the other hand. "Shoo-shoo baby boy."

"See, I can hear you talking to my dog, you aberration, so why don't you come out here and talk to me?"

Vic stood a few feet inside the front door, leaving it open behind him. "Come on, motherfucker, come get me."

In response, the bedroom door flew off its hinges. Vic sped out the front door. New-Vic, girded into a sloppy attack, extended the sword forward like a javelin lance as he advanced on his enemy. He cleared the front door's threshold just as Norman's blade cleaved the air and sliced into his neck. New-Vic screamed, dropped forward, torso hitting the railing, head hanging by threads. Vic sliced through them with ease, and the head plummeted toward the pool . . .

. . . where Cozy, happily treading water in the deep end, glanced up at the still screaming disembodied head before it plunged in the water inches from her. Everything learned about how the body naturally wants to stay afloat vanished from her shrieking brain as she sank, watching the head float to the bottom and trying not to gulp pool water.

Mamie dove in, swam to Cozy, and pulled her to the shallow end, while Yeong-jin attempted to fish the head out with the pool strainer.

Victor Moss, man of action, dropped his weapon, and with one hand, he cleared the second-story railing to cannonball into the deep end, something he'd always dreamed of doing, albeit to a chorus of hotties cheering him on. The head settled on the pool drain, eyes open and dead-seeming, mouth still in the shape of a scream. He snagged it by the hair and swam to the shallow end, emerging with the cocky 'tude of a hero who'd finally conquered the monster. On his trek upstairs, Vic didn't look or speak to anyone. But once he stepped over the clone's body, he understood how this might've looked to the gals and guys downstairs.

"Sorry if I freaked you out," he shouted over the railing. "It was an unsuccessful experiment, nothing to worry about, nothing I'll ever do again, nothing to fix." He spied a pool of pink blood by the clone's feet, and the trail of blood courtesy Vic had created by transporting the head. "And a little bit of clean-up. Congrats, Cozy and Jun! Sorry times a thousand. It'll never happen again." He put hand to heart, but since the hand was holding a head, the gesture was hardly reassuring.

Nobody responded. Each attempted a facial expression other than abject terror as Vic nodded goodbye, placed the head on the body's torso, and dragged it all into his apartment.

"No ribs for that gida," Yeong-jin said.

***

Pulling the body into the kitchen, Vic knew he didn't want the moral of his tale to be that it was permissible to kill robots, although, in a kill-or-be-killed situation, a guy had no choice. Rather, With goals in place, personal accountability, and the doggedness to overcome and correct oft-wavering discipline, a person can surmount all problems, big or small.

The clone's unblinking eyes seemed to watch Vic as he let go of the feet. The thing had been running around town in slippers. Idiot. He removed its clothes like a proper graverobber—fast, thorough, no dilly dallying, except for ten seconds of silent reverence at its penis, his penis. His first view of his own penis from an objective perspective that wasn't captured on a cell phone camera. Not bad. eightieth percentile, easy.

37.
SEVERAL MONTHS LATER

LOS ANGELES BLEW into a flowering spring, with lavish vegetation on hills that would incinerate during fire season.

Vic got a prosthetic eyelid, and it looked almost real, if a little off-color. He framed the eyepatch so it might always be displayed on the bookshelf alongside Riker and Paps.

Friends of Jun-ho and Yeong-jin purchased *Killing It*. Vic made enough to put a sizeable down payment on a condo in Tujunga, a grittier area than Montrose, with fewer cutesy shops and more superstores and car repair joints.

***

New wood inlays sealed cracks in the coffee table trunk. The suit of armor stood on its mount by a groovy gas fireplace. The Hoo Maru, the Japanese prints, and the sword display looked swell on the condos' high walls. *Lovers in a Garden* hung up in the second-story bedroom loft.

Between the dancing flames and the velvety soundtrack of Harry Styles' new Cole Porter covers album, the atmosphere reeked of romance. Darla, the HR lady, ambled around the room, admiring Vic's doodads and gimcracks. She wore a lovely dress and had her hair up. Vic spent a lot of time imagining himself nuzzling her long neck.

Vic set a charcuterie board onto the bistro table.

"Mmm!" Darla abandoned the stack of LPs to investigate the food.

Vic cut her a piece of cheddar. She opened her mouth, and he placed it on her tongue. "Body of Christ." Darla shot him a flirty look, foretelling future coupling.

"Look at this." He licked the cheese knife clean, then placed it on his prosthetic eyelid, where it stuck. "Huh?" He swung it back and forth. "I'm magnetic."

She giggled. "Can you do that with a sword?"

"In a pinch, maybe."

"This is both sinister and interesting," she said, walking over to the suit of armor. "Young goth me is swooning somewhere back in time."

The move prickled Vic's skin. He would have dragged it upstairs, but it was over a hundred pounds. "It's a 14th-century replica from the early twentieth century."

"Where did you find it?"

"In a warehouse outside of downtown." He threw a furtive glance at the coffee table trunk, where Number One was sniffing around. What Darla didn't know was that inside, wrapped in nine yards of saran wrap and duct tape, dwelled the head of the clone, in repose as though sleeping. Vic hadn't the stomach to dismember and scatter the parts in the National Forest or the desert, so logged it as a failed goal and got out the trusty duct tape.

Darla poked the breastplate. "Hey lunkhead!" She raised the helmet's visor. "You have a mouth in here?"

"You want some gouda?" Vic said, slathering some on a cracker and trying not to worry. "It's gouda."

She rolled her eyes, "Ouch, Vic." Her eyes twinkled at him when she laughed. But he couldn't enjoy it; he had to get her to abandon the suit of armor inspection because if she were two inches taller or stood on her toes, she'd see a neck stump covered in saran wrap, which would be so, so, *so* unconducive to a sexy evening.

***

LIKE REAL

Back-lit by a low-hung moon, Cord's warehouse appeared as a gargantuan monolith, a vast slab of darkness. No cars in front. No lights in the cracks—until the front doors parted, and out stepped Stephan, a silhouette in front of the bright reception lights. He threw back his less misshapen head, teeth and jaw in their proper places, raising his eyes to the star-less sky. His left eye hummed as it detached from its socket, rising 350 feet before rocketing in a north-by-northwest direction.

***

Vic and Darla were old-timey fox-trotting to "Love for Sale" and didn't hear the humming outside the window.

But Number One heard and scuttled upstairs.

The head in the trunk opened its eyes.

The clone body in the suit of armor stepped off its mount.

Darla screamed; Vic ran to fetch a katana.

The suit of armor clanked over to the trunk, raised its ax, and cleaved the trunk into two.

As Vic drove forward with his blade, bellowing "ken-ten-tai-chi," he wondered if he and Darla would still be in play after the battle to come.

ACKNOWLEDGEMENTS

Thanks to my buddy Sabrina Kaleta, who savvied me to John Skipp, a writing hero and wellspring of goodwill and wisdom, whose excellent class (and ongoing notes) helped transform my *Like Real* screenplay into a book. His class is where I met Brian Asman, dispenser of great feedback and creator of spectacular prose that blew my mind and made me work harder. Thanks also to my partner, Ron Lynch, a saint of a dude who I love who listened to me read chapters and elucidate my worries about mediocre sentences. And to my friend Steve Robles, a regular idea sherpa, for his cracking beta reading skills and positivity.

Since I'm here, I'd also like to shout out Max and Lori for making my first experience in the publishing world feel so pleasant and kind and enthusiastic and full of passionate people doing good work. Also, to Angie Clark, the BFF since fifth grade who told me in all seriousness that she would force her children to promote my work. She's a righteous freak and everyone should be so lucky to have one of her in their life. Also to Mike Dennis and Dennis Mahoney, who I adore. You guys have given me so much feedback and so many free dinners, I'll always be grateful.

ABOUT THE AUTHOR

Shelly is a nice lady from Los Angeles who considers herself a real LA townie. Her favorite TV movies are *The Initiation of Sara, Mansquito, Yeti: Curse of the Snow Demon,* and Lifetime's *Killer Under the Bed,* the *best* movie about evil sentient dolls.

As an entertainment journalist, she interviewed Roger Corman and once angered Burt Reynolds by asking him what he learned about directing from working with Paul Thomas Anderson. Now she knows Reynolds directed at least nine movies and wishes to apologize to him, wherever he is.

She wrote screenplays for unsavory characters and marketing copy for a big search engine before reinventing herself as a narrative prose writer. Perhaps you've seen her short stories in anthologies or on her site, shellylyons.com.

If you wish to meet Shelly in her natural habitat, you might find her skulking through various Los Angeles neighborhoods in search of a Little Free Library or standing in line for a double feature at The New Bev.

SPOOKY TALES FROM GHOULISH BOOKS 2023

LIKE REAL | Shelly Lyons

ISBN: 978-1-943720-82-8 $16.95

This mind-bending body horror rom-com is a rollicking Cronenbergian gene splice of *Idle Hands* and *How to Lose a Guy in 10 Days*. It's freaky. It's fun. It's LIKE REAL.

XCRMNTMNTN | Andrew Hilbert

ISBN: 978-1-943720-81-1 $14.95

When a pile of shit from space lands near a renowned filmmaker's set, inspiration strikes. Take a journey up a cosmic mountain of excrement with the director and his film crew as they ascend into madness led only by their own vanity and obsession. This is a nightmare about creation. This is a dream about poop. This is a call to arms against vowels. This is *XCRMNTMNTN*.

BOUND IN FLESH | edited by Lor Gislason

ISBN: 978-1-943720-83-5 $16.95

Bound in Flesh: An Anthology of Trans Body Horror brings together 13 trans and non-binary writers, using horror to both explore the darkest depths of the genre and the boundaries of flesh. A disgusting good time for all! Featuring stories by Hailey Piper, Joe Koch, Bitter Karella, and others.

CONJURING THE WITCH | Jessica Leonard

ISBN: 978-1-943720-84-2 $16.95

Conjuring the Witch is a dark, haunted story about what those in power are willing to do to stay in power, and the sins we convince ourselves are forgivable.

WHAT HAPPENED WAS IMPOSSIBLE | E. F. Schraeder

ISBN: 978-1-943720-85-9 $14.95

Everyone knows the woman who escapes a massacre is a final girl, but who is the final boy? *What Happened Was Impossible* follows the life of Ida Wright, a man who knows how to capitalize on his childhood tragedies . . . even when he caused them.

THE ONLY SAFE PLACE LEFT IS THE DARK|
Warren Wagner
ISBN: 978-1-943720-86-6 $14.95

In *The Only Safe Place Left is the Dark*, an HIV positive gay man must leave the relative safety of his cabin in the woods to brave the zombie apocalypse and find the medication he needs to stay alive.

THE SCREAMING CHILD| Scott Adlerberg
ISBN: 978-1-943720-87-3 $16.95

Scott Adlerberg's *The Screaming Child* is a mystery horror novel told by a grieving woman working on a book about an explorer who was murdered in a remote wilderness region, only to get caught up in a dangerous journey after hearing the distant screams from her own vanished child somewhere in the woods.

RAINBOW FILTH | Tim Meyer
ISBN: 978-1-943720-88-0 $14.95

Rainbow Filth is a weirdo horror novella about a small cult that believes a rare psychedelic substance can physically transport them to another universe.

LET THE WOODS KEEP OUR BODIES| E. M. Roy
ISBN: 978-1-943720-89-7 $16.95

The familiar becomes strange the longer you look at it. Leo Bates navigates a broken sense of reality, shattered memories, and a distrust of herself in order to find her girlfriend Tate and restore balance to their hometown of Eston—if such a thing ever existed to begin with.

SAINT GRIT| Kayli Scholz
ISBN: 978-1-943720-90-3 $14.95

One brooding summer, Nadine Boone pricks herself on a poisonous manchineel tree in the Florida backcountry. Upon self-orgasm, Nadine conjures a witch that she calls Saint Grit. Pitched as *Gummo* meets *The Craft*, Saint Grit grows inside of Nadine over three decades, wreaking repulsive havoc on a suspicious cast of characters in a small town known as Sugar Bends. Comes in Censored or Uncensored cover.

Ghoulish Books
PO Box 1104
Cibolo, TX 78108

☐ LIKE REAL	16.95
☐ XCRMNTMNTN	14.95
☐ BOUND IN FLESH	16.95
☐ CONJURING THE WITCH	16.95
☐ WHAT HAPPENED WAS IMPOSSIBLE	14.95
☐ THE ONLY SAFE PLACE LEFT IS THE DARK	14.95
☐ THE SCREAMING CHILD	16.95
☐ RAINBOW FILTH	14.95
☐ LET THE WOODS KEEP OUR BODIES	16.95
☐ SAINT GRIT	14.95

Censored | Uncensored

Ship to:

Name _____

Address _____

City_____State_____Zip _____

Phone Number _____

Book Total: $_____

Shipping Total: $_____

Grand Total: $_____

Not all titles available for immediate shipping. All credit card purchases must be made online at GhoulishBooks.com. Shipping is 5.80 for one book and an additional dollar for each additional book. Contact us for international shipping prices. All checks and money orders should be made payable to Perpetual Motion Machine.

Christian Books
PO Box 1104
Obola, TX 75104

□ LILAH BRAU 10.95
□ C KERMITMTN 14.95
□ ID BOLIN JJ N FLASH 16.95
□ CONJURING THE WITCH 16.95
□ WHAT HAPPENED WAS IMPOSSIBLE 14.95
□ THE ONLY SAFE PLACE LEFT IS THE DARK .. 11.95
□ THE SCREAMING CHILD 10.95
□ RAINBOW FISH 14.95
□ LETTING GO OUR KEEP OUR BODIES 16.95
□ SAY YCRIT 14.95
Carson & J Threatened

Ship to: _____

Name _____

Address _____

City _____ State __ Zip _____

Phone Number _____

Book Total $ _____

Shipping Total $ _____

Grand Total $ _____

Patreon:
www.patreon.com/pmmpublishing

Website:
www.GhoulishBooks.com

Facebook:
www.facebook.com/GhoulishBooks

Twitter:
@GhoulishBooks

Instagram:
@GhoulishBookstore

Newsletter:
www.PMMPNews.com

Linktree:
linktr.ee/ghoulishbooks